A BOOK OF THE DEAD

BY

JOHN BLACKBURN

I0524462

with a new introduction by
GREG GBUR

VALANCOURT BOOKS

A Book of the Dead by John Blackburn
First published London: Robert Hale, 1984
First Valancourt Books edition 2017

Copyright © 1984 by John Blackburn
Introduction © 2017 by Greg Gbur

Published by Valancourt Books, Richmond, Virginia
http://www.valancourtbooks.com

All Valancourt Books publications are printed on acid free paper that
meets all ANSI standards for archival quality paper.

ISBN 978-1-943910-74-8 (*trade paperback*)
Also available as an electronic book.

Cover design by Kerry Squires
Set in Dante MT

A BOOK OF THE DEAD

JOHN BLACKBURN was born in 1923 in the village of Corbridge, England, the second son of a clergyman. Blackburn attended Hailey-bury College near London beginning in 1937, but his education was interrupted by the onset of World War II; the shadow of the war, and that of Nazi Germany, would later play a role in many of his works. He served as a radio officer during the war in the Mercantile Marine from 1942 to 1945, and resumed his education afterwards at Durham University, earning his bachelor's degree in 1949. Blackburn taught for several years after that, first in London and then in Berlin, and married Joan Mary Clift in 1950. Returning to London in 1952, he took over the management of Red Lion Books.

It was there that Blackburn began writing, and the immediate success in 1958 of his first novel, *A Scent of New-Mown Hay*, led him to take up a career as a writer full time. He and his wife also maintained an antiquarian bookstore, a secondary occupation that would inform some of his work, including the bibliomystery *Blue Octavo* (1963). *A Scent of New-Mown Hay* typified the approach that would come to char-acterize Blackburn's twenty-eight novels, which defied easy categoriza-tion in their unique and compelling mixture of the genres of science fiction, horror, mystery, and thriller. Many of Blackburn's best novels came in the late 1960s and early 1970s, with a string of successes that included the classics *A Ring of Roses* (1965), *Children of the Night* (1966), *Nothing but the Night* (1968; adapted for a 1973 film starring Christo-pher Lee and Peter Cushing), *Devil Daddy* (1972) and *Our Lady of Pain* (1974). Somewhat unusually for a popular horror writer, Blackburn's novels were not only successful with the reading public but also won widespread critical acclaim: the *Times Literary Supplement* declared him 'today's master of horror', while the *Penguin Encyclopedia of Horror and the Supernatural* regarded him as 'certainly the best British novelist in his field' and the *St James Guide to Crime & Mystery Writers* called him 'one of England's best practicing novelists in the tradition of the thriller novel'.

By the time Blackburn published his final novel in 1985, much of his work was already out of print, an inexplicable neglect that continued until Valancourt began republishing his novels in 2013. John Blackburn died in 1993.

By John Blackburn

★ Available from Valancourt Books.   † Forthcoming.

INTRODUCTION

The book you are currently holding in your hands, John Blackburn's 1984 novel *A Book of the Dead*, is simultaneously the rarest of his numerous works as well as one of the most familiar. This may at first seem paradoxical, but it turns out that *A Book of the Dead* is a reworking of one of Blackburn's earliest novels, *Blue Octavo* (1963), which was written at what was arguably the height of his career. The two books, though almost identical in plot, are nonetheless strikingly different, as we will see.

John Blackburn had a long and prolific career as an author, though it took him some years to settle into that profession. Born in 1923 in Corbridge, England, Blackburn worked a variety of jobs before officially putting pen to paper. Through the years, he served as a lorry driver, a schoolmaster in London, and a teacher in Berlin. He attended two different colleges, with his studies interrupted in the interim by World War II. During the war, he served as a radio officer in the Mercantile Marine. He also worked as the director of a bookstore in London, and it was during that time that he wrote and published his first novel, the biological horror story *A Scent of New-Mown Hay*, in 1958. The book was a critical and commercial success, and Blackburn was buoyed by it to write some thirty novels total, the last being the science fiction/horror tale *The Bad Penny* (1985).

Even though he was turning out roughly a novel a year, Blackburn also managed to operate an antiquarian bookstore with his wife. It is from this work that he was evidently inspired to write the 1963 book *Blue Octavo*, an ingenious mystery which is set in the eccentric and unpredictable world of rare booksellers. When an aging bookseller named Roach is found dead, an apparent suicide, after spending an absurd amount of money on an obscure and worthless limited edition rock-climbing book, his friend John Cain suspects foul play. Further investigation uncovers that multiple copies of the book, *The Grey Boulders*, have been purchased, stolen, or destroyed in recent months, and that a number of people connected with the book have been found dead in curious circumstances. Cain, with the help of lovely industry heiress Julia Lent and eccentric and egotistical adventurer J. Moldon Mott, vows to root out and expose the murderous bibliophobe, but this act makes him into a target, as well. Can the trio uncover the secret of the book before the murderer strikes again, at book or person?

A Book of the Dead follows the same broad plot, and superficially is essentially the same story. When an aging bookseller named Pike is found dead, an apparent suicide, after spending an absurd amount of money on an obscure and worthless limited edition book of true adventure tales, his friend Tom Mayne suspects foul play. Further investigation uncovers that multiple copies of the book, *Men of Courage*, have been purchased, stolen, or destroyed in recent months, and that a number of people connected with the book have been found dead in curious circumstances. Mayne, with the help of lovely industry heiress Janet Vale and eccentric and egotistical adventurer J. Moldon Mott, vows to root out and expose the murderous bibliophobe, but this act makes him into a target, as well. Can the trio uncover the secret of the book before the murderer strikes again, at book or person?

A Book of the Dead is indeed very much the same as *Blue Octavo*, and is certainly a very close rewrite of that earlier book. For example, we can compare the first paragraph of Chapter 4 of both. From *Blue Octavo*, we have:

> Five minutes after John had opened his shop that morning he received a phone call from the Metropolitan Library. It was a long, tortuous call with Mr Reade's voice slurring and stuttering at the end of the line, but when he finally replaced the receiver his eyes were very thoughtful. Part of his theory was beginning to come up, it seemed. Somebody with a very strange or abnormal mind was interested in *Grey Boulders*.

And from *A Book of the Dead*, we have:

> Five minutes after Tom opened his shop the next morn-
> ing, he received a telephone call from the Walpole Library. A
> long, rambling call with Mr Jason Biggs slurring on the end
> of the line. But when he finally replaced the receiver, Tom's
> eyes were very thoughtful. At least, part of his suspicions
> were true, it seemed. Somebody with an extremely strange
> and abnormal mind was interested in *Men of Courage*.

The two books are not exactly the same, however, and fans of
Blackburn will be well-served to read both. First of all, and most
importantly, it should be noted that the secret of the blue octa-
vos of the two novels are very, very, different from each other,
and lead to very different climactic scenes. As Blackburn's books
are very short and fast-paced reads, it is worth the cost of admis-
sion, so to speak, simply to get to read another Blackburn twist.

Also, Blackburn's novels share a cast of rotating and recurring characters, and *A Book of the Dead* is updated to include
a number of those. Major-General Charles Kirk, who first
appeared as the protagonist in *A Scent of New-Mown Hay*, plays
the role of an investigator trying to close a case that has haunted
him for decades. Also appearing is Peggy Tey, the former partner of criminal Bill Easter, who shared adventures together in
Deep Among the Dead Men (1973), *Mister Brown's Bodies* (1975), *The
Cyclops Goblet* (1977), and *A Beastly Business* (1982). By *A Book of
the Dead*, the duo has finally parted ways, and Peggy Tey makes
a brief appearance early in the novel to spur the investigation.

The most significant recurring character, however, is the
obnoxious J. Moldon Mott – adventurer, eccentric, author,
and amateur crime-fighter. Mott first appeared to save the day
in Blackburn's first spy thriller, *Dead Man Running* (1960), and
would show up to fight subterranean psychics in *Children of
the Night* (1966), as well as werewolves in the aforementioned
A Beastly Business. Of course, he also appeared in *Blue Octavo*,
and he plays the same role in *A Book of the Dead*: drawn into the
intrigue by pure coincidence, he becomes convinced that only

he can solve the mystery, and volunteers himself for the mission. His adventures play out somewhat differently in the later book, and Blackburn gives him a professional nemesis to butt heads with. Mott is, in my opinion, Blackburn's greatest character creation: an obnoxious, egotistical, self-aggrandizing lout, but a man who is fearlessly brave and has an unwavering sense of righteousness.

A Book of the Dead was Blackburn's second-to-last novel, and his final work – *The Bad Penny* (1985) – is also a close reworking of an earlier book. *The Bad Penny* is a rewrite of Blackburn's second novel, *A Sour Apple Tree* (1958), a supernatural thriller in which Nazi experimentation has produced a psychic monster with the potential to destroy the world. This rewrite, like *A Book of the Dead*, has also been updated to modern times and with a revised roster of recurring characters. Charles Kirk appears in both books, but in the more recent one he is now retired and investigating threats with limited governmental resources and a weakened physique. Bill Easter has been added to *The Bad Penny*, having been drafted into service with Kirk, more or less against his will. The Nazi threat has also been revised somewhat, to take into account that 40 years have passed since World War II and any surviving Nazis must be getting quite ancient!

A natural question to ask: why would Blackburn rewrite and repackage his classic works in this way? He was evidently not a man with a limited imagination, as his lengthy bibliography can attest. Unfortunately, Blackburn was a rather private man and did not do many, if any, interviews about his work, so we don't have any definite answers to the question.

A few possibilities come to mind, none of which are mutually exclusive. Blackburn may have gotten into a dispute with his first publisher about the rights to his books, the earliest of which were certainly out of print by 1984. By making the books just different enough to avoid legal issues, he could rerelease them to a new audience that likely had not read the decades-old originals. Another possibility is that Blackburn simply wanted to update the stories for modern times, with better writing skills that he had developed over 30 years of experience. The significant changes that he made in particular to the climax and mystery in *A Book of the Dead* suggests that he felt the original revelations needed improvement. Finally, some of the few biographical sketches of Blackburn that exist suggest that his health was failing in the last years of his life, which ended in 1993. He may have only had the energy and focus to do revisions of existing stories, rather than craft entirely new ones.

In any case, Blackburn's last two novels actually do something surprising for the dedicated reader that Blackburn himself probably did not intend. Their depictions of the same events happening again, decades later, provide a surreal sense of history repeating itself. In Blackburn's universe, enemies can be defeated, and threats eliminated, but new ones will inevitably appear. Civilization, and humanity itself, is always on the brink of destruction in Blackburn's stories. The repetition of *The Bad Penny*, in particular, drives home this idea.

These final two novels also give a sense of closure, a last hurrah of sorts, for many of the characters. We get a last, updated look at Charles Kirk, Bill Easter, and J. Moldon Mott, and in some cases get a glimpse at their ultimate fates. *A Bad Penny* and *A Book of the Dead*, though derivative, gives the dedicated Blackburn fan a chance to say farewell to the characters, and to the brilliant author himself.

GREG GBUR
June 18, 2017

GREG GBUR is a professor of physics and optical science at the University of North Carolina at Charlotte. He writes the long-running blog 'Skulls in the Stars', which discusses classic horror fiction, physics, and the history of science, as well as the curious intersections between the three topics. His science writing has been featured in 'The Best Science Writing Online 2012,' published by Scientific American, and his horror writing has appeared in a number of volumes of the literary horror magazine *Dead Reckonings*. He has previously introduced several John Blackburn novels for Valancourt Books.

One

"Well, gentlemen, shall we proceed to the slaughter?" Officially the sale was over. The auctioneer had brought down his hammer for the last time and Jack Isaacs grinned at the porters who were starting to shift the lots. The boys grinned at each other and sidled towards the door. The real business was about to begin.

They slunk down the path like soldiers fearing ambush. Not in a group, which might suggest conspiracy, but in shambling twos and threes. Hats and caps pulled low over pallid, crafty faces. Grubby fingers clutching catalogues. Furniture dealers into a van parked on the drive. Booksellers towards the damp garden. Twelve men standing around a rose bed and preparing to bid for goods they had already bought. The ring going into action.

"A mixed day, gentlemen, so let's get it over with." Jack Isaacs took up his position on a flagstone square and scowled at the late spring sky. Late spring already, with the buds coming out on the trees and a few crocuses showing. The boys weren't interested in spring or buds or flowers. They stared at their well marked catalogues and waited. Thirty lots had been sold to three of their members for a song while the others kept quiet. Good business, for why should dog eat dog? Now the legal owners would put them up for sale again and the knock-out reveal their true value. Books for those who wanted them and a share of the kitty for the rest.

"Yes, we are all present, gentlemen, and I shall proceed." Jack Isaacs, the ringleader, might have been opening a charitable sale of work and he leaned back against a sundial and consulted his catalogue. "Number twelve was the first lot we bought and it was sold to Mr Barton for twenty pounds. What may I start at please?

"Thank you, Mr Algar; fifty then. Mr Mayne; seventy. Mr Grasper; seventy-five. Any more, gentlemen? Yours for seventy-five, Bill, leaving us with fifty-five as a dividend.

"Now, let's turn to Number twenty-three. The collection of hunting prints, which, owing to the intervention of that very trying young woman in the fur coat, forced Mr Smith to go up to fifty. Thank you, Mr Lehman, I have eighty then . . ."

Slowly and quietly, without excitement or rancour, the transactions proceeded, for what was there to be rancorous about? Nobody could lose. Books for the highest bidders and a cut of the kitty for those who couldn't match the offer or merely kept quiet. Quite a nice little kitty. Sometimes the difference between what a lot had reached in the official auction was multiplied three times by the ring. All very friendly and respectable. It was only when Isaacs reached the end of his catalogue that a note of bitterness crept into the proceedings.

"Sixty pounds, Mr Isaacs." Jonathan Pike stood a little apart from the other gentlemen, and against a background of trees and vegetation he didn't look like a gentleman. He looked like an illustration from a book of folk tales. A sinister gnome waiting to tempt the lost traveller in one of the Grimm brothers' grimmer fairy stories.

"All right, eighty it is, Mr Goldsmith."

Eighty quid! Though Pike spoke confidently Tom Mayne knew that it was not all right and glanced at the notes on his catalogue. Lot One hundred and five; three books on sailing and navigation. *The Loss of the Cospatrick*, *A Million Ocean Miles* and *Men of Courage*. They had only fetched a tenner at the sale and eighty was absurd. Neither Pike nor Goldsmith would have a customer to pay that sort of money for them.

"Eighty-five", "Ninety-five", "One hundred". No, not just absurd; quite crazy. Tom knew that Pike and Goldsmith were enemies, of course. Carrying the scars of some unsatisfactory piece of business down through the years, but could they be throwing money away just for spite, though that had to be the reason. At the very outside, thirty was the maximum figure, and he had marked that price in his catalogue.

"One hundred and ten." "And twenty." All the same why should he worry? Not his or any other man's business if the two bitter old fools wanted to cut their own throats. Tom glanced at Peter Barton of the *Farman Bookshop* and winked. The harder Pike and Goldsmith fought over that trashy lot, the more pickings there would be for the rest of them. The sale itself had been a washout. Too few books amongst too many dealers, but the dividend should make the day worthwhile. "One fifty." "And eighty." "Two hundred." Far away down the drive Tom heard the sound of lorries and porters' barrows. The furniture boys had completed their affairs, had divided the cut and were loading up. They'd run their own ring in a comfortable van, unlike the poor booksellers shivering in the cold.

"Another fifty, Mr Goldsmith." Sam Isaacs beamed. A wicked uncle trying to lure the orphaned nephew into squandering his fortune, and the bidder nodded, though Tom sensed this was his top limit. The man's expression was quite blank apart from a slight air of smugness.

Goldsmith had not wanted the books himself. He wasn't a specialist on any of the subjects. He had no customer who would pay that kind of money for them, but he somehow knew that Pike had. Somehow, through some tortuous little channel he'd discovered that, and he'd driven old Pike up to the last gasp, the final level. Tom watched him light a cigarette and turn away as though the whole business had become distasteful to him.

"Mr Pike. I have two hundred and fifty pounds and it is against you." Isaacs still beamed, but there was something cautious about his expression. He probably suspected that Pike was out of his mind, but he wasn't sure. Old Pike had been in the trade a long, long time and was supposed to know his business. Could there be something about that lot he'd missed? Something which made the books valuable. Jack

Isaacs hated the thought of missing anything of value. He was 70 years old himself, with a hundred thousand pounds worth of stock tucked away in the basement of his shop, but the idea of missing a bargain still gave him nightmares. Rows and rows and miles and miles of priceless books trickling away into other people's stores and lists of catalogues, and not a single volume for poor Jackie Isaacs.

No, impossible. He'd checked carefully. He always checked carefully. There was no interesting inscription to give any of the books an inflated value. *The Cospatrick* and *The Million Miles* were only worth a few quid and in pretty poor condition. *Men of Courage* was a limited edition of course, but worth ten at the outside. The very outside, and two fifty was ridiculous. Pike was a senile fool, and Goldsmith realized that and had driven him up for the hell of it. Well, if Pike wanted to throw good money away, the best of British luck to him.

"The bidding is against you at two and a half, Mr Pike," he said. "May I hear a further offer?"

"Three then." Isaacs didn't hear anything. He saw. Pike nodded, he lifted his finger and the hammer came down. The barter was over and all that remained were three things. Collect the money – hand over the purchases and divide the lolly amongst the boys who had only stood and waited.

"I showed him, Tommy. I showed bloody Goldsmith where he got off." Pike climbed into Tom's car with the three books under his arm. "I showed the bastard where he got off, didn't I?" He untied the string holding his hoard together and placed two of them on the shelf. "Them couple is for you, boy. A sort of token of thanks for running me about to the sales now and again and you're very welcome."

"Thanks, Mr Pike, but I still don't understand why." Tom glanced at the two volumes and then at his passenger's little monkey-muzzled face. Though he and Pike had been friends for years he still called him Mister; there was so much age difference between them.

"I don't understand a thing. You didn't show Goldsmith up. He ran you up and don't ask me why you let him.

"Sam had no use for those books and he stopped bidding exactly when the time was ripe. He made you pay about fifteen times over the odds for one volume and I'm curious to know the reason. Did you go crazy and cut off your nose for the sake of Sam Goldsmith?"

"Maybe, Tommy, but why should you complain?" Pike's voice was strange, tinged with cockney, and another accent Tom did not recognize. "Yes, maybe I wanted to do Sam in the eye but so what? An eye for an eye and a tooth for a tooth as his father might have said and I'll tell you about it . . ."

"I've already heard the story, Mr Pike." Tom remembered the tale well. Four or five years ago Goldsmith had asked Pike to send him a copy of *Bewick's Birds* on approval. The book had been returned labelled "imperfect" which it definitely was by then. Three plates had been removed and transferred into another copy owned by honest Sam Goldsmith. "But though Sam's maybe a crook he's proved you a bloody fool, and those books on the glove tray suggest he's right," Tom said. "Why did you hand over a fortune for that *Men of Courage?*"

"I honestly don't know, Tommy. I haven't a clue, but there's something special about it all right; to one person anyway." Pike held the book out to him. "Have a squint yourself and try to tell me."

"Thanks." Tom tilted the book into the light and looked at the cover. He'd never actually handed a copy of *Men of Courage*, but he knew about it from catalogues and auction records. A Raeburn Press edition on well-known heroics, amply illustrated and limited to a hundred and fifty copies. Published some years after the Second World War and issued to private subscribers and admirers of the heroes.

He turned the pages and saw a few of the personalities performing the feats which had earned them fame. Blondin balanced on a rope across Niagara Falls. Matthew Webb prepared to make his first swim across the English Channel. Colonel Cody, Buffalo Bill, with his boots, his rifle and his flowing moustache. Flight-Lieutenant Learoyd with his VC awarded *"for most conspicuous bravery"*.

A nice book, Tom supposed, but not all that nice. The binding was slightly loose, the paper showed signs of foxing and the print was too flamboyant. Not a volume worth anything like three hundred pounds except to a maniac, and he pushed it across to the maniac who'd bought it.

"Well I've looked," he said, "and there's nothing special about the thing in my opinion. If I wanted to throw money away I'd rather back a slow horse or a dog with arthritis."

"Yes, I suppose you might, son, but you'd be wrong – very wrong." Pike lit a cigarette as Tom started the car and they drove off. "I was wrong once you know. Years ago, before I'd really started to specialize, I found an *Atlantic Neptune* in a junk-shop. That eighteenth-century book on seamanship is a good, valuable work, as you know, but mine was in a mess. Some blasted child had scribbled over all of the margins and the plates in thick black ink. Couldn't get 'em out, so I offered it to Saul Victorious of New York for a song. Saul was only over here for a while, but he paid up and went away to do his homework. Spent several hours at the Naval and War museums and identified the child responsible. I never found out what Saul made out of that transaction, but it couldn't have been less than a quarter of a million dollars. The blasted scribbler was a Mr Midshipman Horatio Nelson.

"Oh, you can laugh, Tommy. I was a blamed, idle fool and I got all I deserved from the deal." Pike spoke with the cigarette dangling from his lips, and he fondled his purchase in an oddly sensuous manner. "But I'm not a fool where this joker is concerned, and I wouldn't part with it for under a thousand."

"A thousand pounds!" Tom gasped. Pike really was round the bend, he thought. There was no sense in what the man said, and the idea of anyone paying that kind of money for *Men of Courage* was a pipe-dream; a delusion.

Yes, a fool's paradise produced by loneliness and he did live alone with only books for companions. That was bound to tell in the end, and the end couldn't be far off now. The old boy was well over 70, but what had he been in the beginning? He had no relatives or close friends and no one knew a thing about his background. The brain was running down, and soon he'd finish up in a home or an asylum, if the decline continued.

"If you've got customers like that I'd hang onto them till grim death," he said.

"I'll hang on, Tommy boy, and you can rely on that." A senile chuckle broke from Pike's lips without disturbing the cigarette. "One has to hang on to good clients in my kind of business – purely catalogue and postal trade.

"Quite different for you with your bright little shop, of course, because you meet people. They come in to browse and have a chat, and sometimes they buy or sell to you. A friendly, personal relationship can build up after a while, but not in my case.

"No, a poor old sod like me has only a telephone and a type-writer to rely on. There's no relationship, because he hardly ever meets the individuals he's dealing with. They're just names on a mailing list, and if I don't give 'em what they want they'll find someone who can.

"And now you can drop me off, Tommy." He watched a bus-stop coming up and smiled. "Thanks for the ride and the chat, but I'll find me own way home from here.

" 'Bye for now, son." The car had stopped and Pike climbed out, but he didn't join the bus queue at first. As soon as Tom was out of sight he walked into a telephone booth and dialled a number.

Home was a ground-floor flat near Norwood Junction, but it wasn't much to write home about. The outside paint was peeling, the brickwork needed pointing and the hall stank of cats, curry and other odours of the East.

But Pike regarded it as home. The place was private and suited him well. He kept his own quarters in good condition and paid his rent regularly. He caused no trouble and was regarded as a model tenant by the Anglo-Indian who owned the building. He unlocked the front door and entered his domain.

Books – everywhere there were books. They lined every wall from floor to ceiling. They were piled against the windows and in the centre of each room. They smelled of must and damp and leather polish, and only three places were unoccupied by them; his kitchen, his bathroom and his bed.

"Now, let's have a look at you," he said, moving to a table and tilting aside a heavy volume to make way for *Men of Courage*. "Tell me your real secret. What makes you so special, my sweet?" He spoke to himself and his voice sounded quite different. All the cockney accent had vanished and it was a cultured and rather academic voice. "They all think I'm mad, but you know they're wrong though you can't tell me why." He slipped a piece of paper into his typewriter and stared at the keys.

"Re: our telephone conversation of this afternoon," he wrote at last. "I confirm that I have a copy of the book in question to hand and ready for you to collect. Very good condition . . ."

He considered the price and then opened a drawer and pulled out his paper-knife, though not to cut paper. The thing was a German officer's dirk and a treasured possession. Gold engravings on both sides of the blade; crossed anchors on one, the imperial crown and eagles glinting on the other.

"Limitation Number is 68," he typed. "My price is . . ." He paused again and thought of what he had told Tom Mayne. He closed his eyes and twirled the dagger. "Let's see what Kaiser Wilhelm can advise, if anything. He spun the blade and saw that the crown emblem was facing him. He dropped the dirk onto the desk and wrote "fifteen hundred pounds".

"You're quite a rare book, but there's nothing really remarkable about you, my sweet. So what makes you so special?" he repeated. "Just what is your true secret? Why are you worth that kind of money? I don't know. I haven't a clue, and I don't suppose I'll ever find out, though it would be interesting to discover the truth one day."

He leaned back in his chair, thinking of the problem with his eyes fixed on the book. He looked half asleep when the door bell rang and with shuffling old-man's footsteps he went to answer it.

Tom Mayne didn't see or think about Pike for two days till a film designer named Perkins rang him up on the subject of Regency Costume. Mr Perkins was a stout, jovial man on the surface but his body housed an aching soul. He was either up to his eyes in work or out of it, and constantly in a hurry.

"No, no, no, Mr Mayne. I've got a set of Townsend, but that deals only with female attire and is no help to me whatsoever. It's the male sex I'm after and what can you suggest?" His voice came in gasps and Tom almost imagined he had been pursuing the sex in question.

"No, no, that's no good at all. I realize you might get some material by advertising in your trade journal, but that won't help me. It takes ten days and I need the books now; immediately. Money, within reason, is no object, but I must have a set of accurate drawings ready by tomorrow at the latest."

"I'll do my best, Mr Perkins, but I'm making no promises." Tom replaced the receiver hurriedly, though he sympathized with his customer's predicament. Commercial television directors were harsh taskmasters, but not eastern potentates who could have one beheaded at the wink of an eye, as Perkins seemed to imagine.

Still it would be pleasant to help poor Mr Perkins and earn some money, and there were several dealers who might have the material. He considered them and then settled for Pike.

Not that Pike would have any works which might be useful. He specialized in sport, aviation, mountaineering and tales of derring-do, but he knew about other people's stock. His memory for titles was like a computer and two thirds of his time was spent wandering about the bookshops in the hope of finding something in his own field. If the material to save Mr Perkins from poverty and ruin was in London, Pike would know where it was and Tom lifted the receiver again.

Damn Pike! The only response to the call was a dull screaming sound. The old fool must have left his receiver off the hook or failed to pay the bill. Might be home though ... Might find him in, and why not? Wednesday – half closing day and it would be nice to get out for a while. His assistant, a dim-witted but very reliable girl of 17 could take care of any passing customers. He told her not to buy anything in his absence and went out.

Pike lived in South Norwood below the slopes of Beulah Hill and no one could have called his residence attractive. A tall Edwardian house which looked as though it would soon be condemned or taken over by the Council as unfit for multiple accommodation. Children played around the dustbins in the front garden, the stench of the hall was horrible and Mr Perkins would have to pay for his costumes, Tom decided. Pay through the nose.

But at least Pike was there, or soon would be, though he didn't answer his bell. Tom rang three times and then saw that the door was ajar. The old dotard must have taken a nap or gone out on some local errand, but he'd be back soon. Tom pushed the door open and walked in.

"Are you there, Mr Pike?" Tom shouted, but what a life, he thought. To live quite alone with nothing but books for company. Not even a woman to clean up for him and no friends.

But at least, the flat was clean and efficient. Though the curtains were drawn, the windows behind must be open because the drapes swayed, slightly in the breeze. Tom stood and looked around, staring across the room and watching the thin gleams of sunlight mottling the books, and the steel filing cabinet, and the desk and the ...

"So you are there," he said, seeing Pike hunched over the desk and walking towards him. "Sorry to disturb your nap, but I rang the bell and there was no answer. The fact is that I need your advice and hope you can help me." There was still no response and Tom shook Pike's shoulder. Just a gentle shake, more of a touch than anything, but enough. The old, frail body did respond. It twisted further and further forward and then slumped to one side. The knife handle gleamed in his chest like a medallion.

Two

"Suicide, Mr Mayne. No doubt about that in my mind." Inspector Charles Pounder leaned forward and smiled. A very bright, flashing smile and his dark hair might have been plastered down with shoe polish. Though not actually fat, he was as sleek as a sea-lion and Tom had the uncomfortable feeling that if one pricked him, he might burst.

"Yes, it's over a week since your friend Pike died, and it's also quite clear that he committed suicide. My – our investigations have been extremely thorough and the inquest is a foregone conclusion. On the day of that Richmond sale, he was in a most unbalanced frame of mind, as you and several of your colleagues have testified. He was an old and probably very unhappy man living alone and the dagger had been in his possession for years; you told us that, Mr Mayne."

"Dagger – no, it was a German naval dirk of the First World War period." Tom could still see the hilt embedded against Pike's chest. "He collected one or two things like that. There's a rope in his cabinet which belonged to George Mallory."

"Mallory?" Pounder frowned slightly. "Ah, yes, the Everest chap. Fellow who gave his reason for climbing a mountain as, 'Because it's there'. Supposed to be clever, but I can never see the point myself. 'Why did you break into that bank, Bill Sykes?' 'Because it was there, Your Honour'." Pounder gave another flashing smile.

"No, that won't get you very far and we can forget about old Pike. A sad, lonely man who acted very strangely at that sale, or the unofficial version which followed it." Pounder clicked his teeth in mock disapproval. "Nothing definitely illegal about a knockout I suppose, but a trifle unsporting, shall we say, and fatal in the case of old Pike.

"He paid ten times more for three items than they were

worth, and two of them he didn't want, seeing he gave them to you. When he gets home from the bus with that one purchase he begins to realize his mind is cracking up and decides to make an end of things. He has the means to hand and he uses it. To fall on his sword." Pounder used the expression with relish. "A popular recreation in Roman and Old Testament times and a stage direction frequently delivered by playwrights. That's about all there is to say, Mr Mayne. An unpleasant way to terminate life, but typical, I'm afraid. Old people living on their own will do anything."

"I suppose so." Tom turned away from Pounder's complacent smile and pushed his mind back. Back to the day of the sale with Pike bidding self-confidently. Back to the drive home and Pike's words, "I'll hang on, Tommy."

"All the same, Inspector," he said. "When I dropped him off at the bus-stop he didn't behave like a man who was planning to kill himself."

"I'm sure that's true, sir, but have you personally met many suicides, and who knows what happened afterwards? You put him down about six o'clock and the medical evidence suggests that he died around nine.

"Just suggests of course. It was two days later that you found him and one can't be accurate after such a long period. But a lot can happen during three hours." Pounder's voice was still polite, but he was clearly becoming bored with Tom's suspicions. "And if you'll take my advice, Mr Mayne, don't even consider the idea of foul play. We found not the slightest suggestion of it and if we had done . . ." He broke off and opened the drawer of his desk. "Yes, if we'd found any suggestion that Pike was murdered you'd probably be in a cell right now."

"I?" Tom flushed slightly. "Why, Inspector? I was quite fond of old Pike. You mean that just because I was with him on the evening he died . . ."

"Because you were with him, sir. Because you found him. Because, to the best of our knowledge, you are the only person with a reason for wishing him dead." He grinned at

Tom's bewilderment and slid a sheet of thick, creamy paper across the desk. "Because of this, Mr Mayne."

"Good God." The thing was a photocopy and as he read its contents, the print seemed to twist and blur before Tom's eyes. "But he never told me – never gave me a hint that he'd done such a thing."

"I'm sure he didn't, Mr Mayne, but that's Pike's will all right. Properly drawn up and witnessed by his solicitors three weeks ago. You are named as his executor and sole heir, and the estate includes a couple of thousand pounds in cash, the lease of his flat, and what I understand is a fairly valuable collection of books.

"Just how valuable is not for me to say, of course, but I can see no reason why you shouldn't inspect your property as soon as possible, Mr Mayne. A bit irregular of course, but I'll take a chance. There's no doubt that the coroner will bring in a verdict of suicide, and the solicitors anticipate no bother about the will.

"Don't sell anything before probate is granted or you'll get me into trouble, but here are the keys." He held them out and his smile flickered over Tom as though awarding him some high honour.

"I think you'll find everything just as you last left it, sir." He raised his hand and the smile faded. "Apart from one dead body, of course."

"And now, Mr Mayne, I've got a lot of work to do and I'm sure you want to examine your inheritance, so goodbye and good luck." He shook Tom's hand and then opened the door for him. He watched him walk away down the corridor and then returned to his desk and lifted a telephone.

"That you, General?" he said when the call was answered. "Charles Pounder here, and though this may not interest you, I'm reporting progress as the super instructed. Just had a chat with Pal Mayne as it happens. Gave him the keys of Pike's flat and tried to put a stop to his ideas of murder.

"What – no." He laughed at the question. "Tom Mayne

wouldn't have the guts to kill anybody himself and it was a clear case of suicide. In my view we can close the file now.

"Thank you, sir. Yes, that is still a point and though we've checked with the records people, they can't help us. Apart from the fact that he used a false name for almost thirty years, we've no idea who Pike really was."

"Suicide – my foot!" Pounder had rung off and the man he had called leaned forward and massaged his hands against an electric fire. The man suffered from cold and, though the room was warm, he was dressed in thick tweeds and wore a pullover. "Suicide," he repeated, partly to himself and partly to his companion. "How many people has that damned book killed to date, Sergeant?" He raised his right hand which lacked three fingers and was mottled with greyish scar tissue. "We don't know, but I'm going to make you a promise. One day, someday, I'll break those bastards and make 'em squirm."

Three

Pounder was wrong. Not everything was as he'd left it. One thing was missing.

Tom sat behind Pike's desk and he'd been there for hours. The ashtray was piled with cigarette stubs and around him lay Pike's correspondence and record books. They told him nothing, or next to nothing. Nothing about his past background. Nothing about his hopes and fears or private feelings. Just notes of business transactions stretching across the years; copies of quotation cards, order forms and invoices. "Dear Sir, We can offer the following." "Thank you for your order, but I regret the book has been sold." "Please send me the copy of *Greener's Gun and Its Development*, as kindly quoted."

Yes, a lot of correspondence. Letters to suppliers and customers. Offers to buyers and enquiries to dealers, but not one single note from a friend or relative. Piles of catalogues and back numbers of the *Clique*. A list of regular clients with their requirements marked beside them. Harold Wilkes Esq. "All on antique guns and pistols." Lord George Lampton. "Back numbers of the Rock and Fell Club Journal." Chief Librarian, University of Boston, Mass. "Manuscript material relating to American or British Sport." Pike had written a great many letters, but nothing about himself or why he had committed suicide with a German dirk.

But Inspector Pounder obviously knew his job. Pike had been old and was slightly unbalanced, and only he, Tom Mayne, had a clear motive for killing him. With Pike's death, he was probably ten thousand pounds better off, so "Why worry?" "Not your business," "Let the dead bury their dead."

And yet he had to be sure. Tom got up and searched the shelves a second time, checking each title against a big bound catalogue in Pike's neat hand, giving the date, price of purchase and what he hoped it would fetch, entered in the margin. Many items had been crossed off and marked "Sold", but one volume had not been entered and it was not on any shelf or on the floor. *Men of Courage* was missing.

Tom finished his search and returned to the desk, lighting another cigarette and trying to concentrate. He had left Pike at roughly six o'clock and he had died around nine. The local post offices shut at five thirty, so he couldn't have posted the book. Had somebody called to collect it?

And just what was interesting about *Men of Courage*? A rather pretentious volume of reminiscences about people who had mostly died years ago. A book worth no more than twenty pounds, for which an eccentric but very old and astute dealer had paid three hundred and claimed he could sell for over a thousand.

Yes, it would be interesting to know the name of the customer who would fork out that kind of money for *Men of Courage*. Plots of half forgotten detective stories started to run through Tom's head. Wills hidden in the spine and incriminating documents stitched among the pages, a map showing the way to buried treasure. Had there been something about that one copy which Pike had spotted?

No, that was unlikely, to say the least. Tom thought of the sale and the knockout which followed. Everybody grinning and gaping as the price went up and up and the boys knew they'd have a dividend beyond their wildest dreams. Pike nodding his head and Goldsmith raising a grimy finger. Yes, Sam Goldsmith must have been sure there was something special about the book. He would never have risked putting Pike up otherwise. Horrid Sam with his bulging face and cunning eyes, like an illustration from a book of animal stories in which the characters have human clothes and occupations. Mr Toad, the dealer, with a great bloated belly poking out above his baggy breeches. It would be interesting to have a word with "Good Old Sam Goldsmith", as he called himself.

"878 78321." The voice which answered the telephone was thick and muddy and sounded as though its owner's mouth was full of food. Tom imagined that that was probably true. Goldsmith must have shut up shop and was tucking into dinner in the room above. Sam had cast off his religious principles years ago, and proved the point by favouring Gentile and highly non-Kosher dishes. Bacon and sausage, and pork chops washed down with mugs of scalding tea.

"Tommy – Tommy Mayne, how kind of you to ring me." The voice changed to a peal of delight as though the call was the one thing that made Goldsmith's day. "And what can I do for you, Tommy? Bought something nice? Want to sell it to me? Well, go ahead. Plenty of cash here and you know I always pay tops for anything in me own line."

"I've heard that, Sam." Goldsmith was one of the meanest payers in the trade and Tom had not been able to discover what his "own line" actually was. On the surface he specialized in history and literature but there were rumours that he had another and more profitable interest. If those rumours were true Goldsmith ran a lending library of expensive smut from the back room of his shop.

"No, Sam, I haven't bought much lately," Tom said. "All the same, I think I have something which might interest you. You see, I've recently been left about three thousand books and I want your help . . ."

"Left – left is it?" The voice rose to a whoop of joy. "Three thousand left to you and you need my help to sort 'em out.

"I appreciate that, Tommy. It's nice to hear a young man pocketing his pride and asking an old stager like me to lend a hand, and of course I'll be delighted. I pay a fair price for anything I can use. Ask anyone in the trade and you'll hear the same thing. 'Good old Sam Goldsmith pays top-notch,' they'll say.

"But what are the books, my boy, and who left 'em to you? Some rich uncle with a taste for leather bindings, maybe?"

"No, not a relative, Sam, and there aren't many bindings.

You might say the library contains mainly military books and a few on sporting subjects."

"Sporting subjects?" The voice became slightly guarded and Tom sensed that Goldsmith was thinking of the rumoured erotica in his back room, then it changed back to excitement again. "You mean – you don't mean old Pike's books, son? He left 'em to you, did he, Tommy. Well, well, the poor old devil. He had no family, so he made you his heir, just because you ran him around to the sales now and then. How crazy can some people get?" He paused for a moment and Tom heard the clink of china. Sam Goldsmith was considering his next move and fortifying himself with a swig of tea.

"And who better should he choose, Tommy? I know how fond you were of Johnny Pike. Always acting like his private chauffeur and putting yerself out for him. Very, very kind you was, and I'm delighted to know he made you his heir. Why, I was only saying to me young lady the other day, 'He's a good friend to Mr Pike, is Tommy Mayne.'

"And you're doing the right thing in coming to me, Tommy. Old Pike would have liked the idea of us sorting through his stock together.

"Oh, I'm not denying that we had our little differences in the past – who hasn't? But deep down we were close as brothers. Like all the trade, he could trust me with his last farthing."

"Then let's get down to business, Sam." Tom cut the eulogy short. "I know you'd give your eye-teeth to look at those books and Pike told me you almost forced your way into his flat on a couple of occasions." He ignored the squeaks of denial on the line and continued. "What was so special about that copy of *Men of Courage* the other day?"

"*Men of Courage*. Ah yes, I remember. You were at the sale, weren't you?" Goldsmith lost all his false friendliness and became more guarded. "What do you want to know about the book, son? It's listed in *Auction Records* and *Book Prices Current*."

"They tell me nothing, Sam, and what I need to know is

this. You and Pike were supposed to be business men, so what happened? Why did you bid over two hundred pounds for three books not worth more than thirty?"

"All right, I'll tell you, son." Goldsmith paused and then his words came out with a rush. "Let me have a few of Pike's books on the cheap and I'll tell you the full story. I thought the old fool had got hold of a *Kamtsen*."

"*Kamtsen!*" Tom remembered the Yiddish word, which could be roughly translated as 'a hoarder'.

"That's right, son, a *Kamtsen*. The crazy collector we dream about like we dream about finding a first of *Alice in Wonderland* or a page from the *Gutenberg Bible*. A man who craves for a certain book and doesn't care what he pays or where it comes from. You often find 'em in the picture trade. Some mad bastard buying a stolen painting he can never show, but gloats over in a cellar. A form of sickness, I suppose, but a bloody profitable form if you can land a rich one."

"Even a poor one is useful, Sam." Tom remembered a customer of his own. A retired clerk living on a pittance who bought copies of a local print at ten guineas a time and was quite frank about his motives. "I can't bear the thought of anybody else owning them, Mr Mayne."

"But *Men of Courage* isn't that kind of book, Sam," he said. "Too general for one thing. If it had just dealt with a single kind of bravery to attract the nut's hero-worship, I could understand, but ..."

"Listen, Tommy, I'm no psychologist, boy. I'm just a poor bloody bookseller and I'll tell you what happened." A chair creaked as Goldsmith shifted his bulk into a more comfortable position. "Four – five months ago Pike came into me shop and spotted a copy of *Men of Courage*. Paid the full trade price and didn't try to haggle, which was unlike him. That didn't really surprise me, but a few days later, I heard he'd bought other copies from Dan Jackson and Archway Books. I pricked my ears up and kept me eyes open as you can imagine."

"I can imagine, Sam." As he listened, a horrible image

appeared in Tom's mind. A great, grey toad with Goldsmith's face, hopping around the alleys in search of scraps.

"Sure I did, Tom. I talked to dealers and porters at the sale-rooms and I read magazines. The *Clique*, *London Daily News* and a dozen others. I found out that Pike was desperate to get hold of that damn book. He'd not only advertised for copies, he'd already bought forty of 'em. Almost a third of the whole edition."

"The devil he had! And you checked this, Sam?"

"I checked all right, Tommy, and when I saw there was a copy for sale at Richmond, I decided to risk a little money. Two hundred and a half I'd go up to for the book and if Pike outbid me, the boys would make a nice profit. If not – if I bought the book I might get my own teeth into Pike's *Kamtsen*."

"Sorry, Sam, But I'm still not with you."

"You should be if you use your head a bit and think about *hoarders*. Them people ain't normal, you know. They crave for things they collect like a drug addict craves for dope. Suppose this man had told Pike to go up to one hundred for the book and Pike lost it. The man would be upset, I think. He would sit at home and feel that he'd just lost his wife or mother, and decide he should have offered more. His crazy mind would tell him that copies, any copy of *Courage* was worth every penny he had to his name and he'd better make some enquiries. Enquiries which would bring him running to me and I'd have a share of Pike's *Kamtsen*."

"I see," Tom said and he really did see how it might have ended. He saw Pike sitting alone with the book and the dirk beside him and waiting for his customer to call. And then, the doorbell rang and he'd got up to admit his customer.

But the customer might have been a poor man, and Pike might have been greedy and asked more than he could afford. Perhaps his sick mind had considered what he had in his wallet, what he owed on the mortgage and what his bank manager had written, and he realized he couldn't pay the price. But all the time that book lay on the table like the Holy Grail and he

knew he had to have it. And as he watched the treasure he had
also seen the key – the means to get it – and his hand had crept
out for the German dirk.

Impossible – no! Tom knew a great deal about collectors
and their cravings and another example came to mind. A
large, florid and happy man who collected copies of the *Lilliput* magazine. "January and May '49, Mr Mayne. Thank you
very much and I only need a dozen to complete the set." His
eyes sparkled as Tom wrapped up the purchases.

Then one day they'd met in the street and Tom hardly recognized his customer, because the man wasn't florid and his
eyes did not sparkle. He'd lost weight too, his body sagged and
he wasn't happy any more.

"*Lilliput*, Mr Mayne," he said. "Oh no, I've got the lot, now,
the full set, and I can relax." What he meant was that all the
fun had gone out of life.

Yes, collectors were a strange breed, and if Pike had found
one who was not strange but ruthless too, if he'd driven the
generous client a little too far, he might have met his killer.

"Thank you, Sam," Tom said into the phone. "That's exactly
what I wanted to know and you can have the first refusal of
any of Pike's books I decide to sell. I'll let you know when to
come round and look at them."

He replaced the receiver and looked round himself. What
he saw almost gave him a heart attack. "A great pleasure to
make your acquaintance, Mr Mayne." The woman was huge.
Sixteen stone if an ounce but, like many large people, she
could move like a cat and had walked silently into the room and
was browsing through the books when Tom spotted her. Her
reddish hair was done up with curlers, she wore pyjamas and
bedroom slippers, her name was Mrs Margaret Tey, but she
soon asked Tom to call her Peggy or Peg for short. She smelled
strongly of Guinness and belched at frequent intervals. She
lived upstairs and knew, or claimed to know, everything.

"Oh yes, me and Mr Pike were very good friends, Mr
Mayne, and I was so very sorry to hear that the poor gentle-

man had gone and done himself in." She prodded one of her bulging breasts with a scarlet fingernail. "To stab himself with that knife. What a way to go, though I suppose one can't blame the poor soul." She hitched her rump onto the desk and sighed soulfully.

"You don't think he did kill himself, Mr Mayne. You believe he may have been murdered. Well, I never!" She belched loudly and Tom drew back from the blast of stout. "I suppose there might be one or two people about with a reason for wanting the old chap dead, but only a handful nowadays, and your notion about a nutty customer doin' 'im in is nonsensical. Oh, I'm not sayin' that there ain't a lot of nutters around, but see for yourself and listen to what Mr Pike told me." She stood up, tightened the cord of her pyjamas and moved across to a pile of magazines. "Surely the name K. 107 rings a bell for you."

"Sounds like a model of a car."

"Well, you're wrong, Mr Mayne. Not a car, but an aircraft. An aircraft which crashed and killed a lot of people." She returned to the desk with a slim volume in her stubby hand and flicked it open. "Here's the joker who got the blame, so have a squint at him."

"Thanks." The magazine was dated 1948 and showed a picture of a slim, bearded man leaning against an airframe. "Mr J.R. Price, designer of the Kingston K.107, taken shortly before the disaster", ran the caption below the print, but even without the beard and the difference in age, Tom recognized the face. "Price, that's who he really was."

"Yes, Mr Price or Mr Pike, what's in a name, though I can only think of him as Pike." She gave another soulful sigh. "The old boy told me the story himself. The K. 107 hit a mountain in Wales during its maiden flight and thirty-three people were killed. Faulty design was to blame and the court of enquiry threw the book at Pike and he was pilloried in the press. Rather like what happened to Sir Thomas Bouch, when the Tay Bridge got blown over. After a while, the poor old bleeder couldn't stand the publicity, so he shaved off his beard, changed his name and became a book runner. Going from shop to shop buying and selling for a few pennies profit. Must have had quite a flair for it, because in no time at all he'd built up a mailing list and dealt with private customers. Aviation material at first, but he soon spread his net further."

"And he told you this himself, Mrs Tey." For the first time Tom seemed to have a clear picture of Pike. That was the reason for the false accent, the loneliness and the hat which he always wore pulled low over his forehead. Even after thirty years those dead passengers and the crew still troubled him.

"Of course he told me, Mr Mayne and why not? Everybody needs a friend to trust and confide in." To Tom's horror, she picked up his hand and fondled it. She then studied the palm. "You need to trust me, too, Mr Mayne, so tell me the truth. Make a clean breast and tell Mummy Peg everything."

And Tom did, though he never knew why. He told the repulsive woman everything he knew; his fears and suspicions. Pike's death had no connection with a long-forgotten aircraft disaster; a book had killed him. A book which had lain on his desk looking quite innocent, though it held a secret which someone was desperate to conceal and would kill for if the need arose. Tom pulled his hand out of Mrs Tey's clammy grasp and considered what might have happened.

Pike was fairly well known as a dealer in his own specialities, and one day he might have had an enquiry by letter or post-card. "I would be glad if you can offer me any copies of *Men of Courage* which may come your way." The writer might either have been a stranger or a regular customer who had been on his list for years.

In any case it was probable that Pike had had at least one copy of the book in stock and had sent it off, and received cash by return. So he had offered the prompt payer more copies, possibly quoting from other dealers' stock, and each offer had been accepted.

Then slowly at first, the price had gone up and up. Tom had

no illusions about Pike's character. If he felt he had a customer with a compulsive urge to buy, he would have put the screws on like a Levantine usurer, and one couldn't blame him for that. The edition was limited to a hundred and fifty copies and a good quarter of those would be stored away in libraries and private collections. Each one he sold would have made the edition a little scarcer and finally he might have believed it was worth what he charged.

"I still think he killed himself, but what are we waiting for, Mr Mayne, and it's worth a try." He had been speaking aloud and Mrs Tey interrupted him and rummaged through the desk. "Here it is; old Pike's list of customers with their wants written down beside 'em."

"We can ignore about half of these of course. No foreigners, and the Bishop of West Auckland is pretty unlikely – his Honour Judge Tenton, Sir Simon Vale, he's chairman of Allied Chemical Engineering, I seem to remember, and they're dead ducks too."

"No, we'll put 'em all in, Mrs Tey. All British residents. A bishop, a judge and an industrialist might have a sick mania for collecting like anybody else." Tom squinted at the first page. A list of fifty names and forty-nine individuals would look at the price and shake their heads, but one might be shocked into action. Always assuming that Pike had included his special customer on the list, of course.

A laborious task, but worth a try. He slipped one of Pike's quotation cards into the typewriter and started work, leaving the bill head intact but writing *successor to* and adding his own address and telephone number below. Then he described the goods he had to sell.

"*Men of Courage* – Fine example, numbered . . ." He couldn't remember the number of Pike's last copy, so selected 50 at random and glanced at his watch. Nearly nine o'clock, but the central post offices had a collection at midnight. If he worked hard he might just make it. The big electric typewriter whirred and clicked under his fingers, the desk light lit him up like a figure on a stage set, the lines of books seemed to frown at him as though he was disturbing their sleep.

He saw Mrs Tey depart to the kitchen and return with two glasses and a bottle of brown liquid, but he tried to ignore her till she patted his shoulder and filled a glass.

"But why your own address, and what price are we goin' to quote?" she asked. "Ah, I see. You may have inherited Pike's money; bloody old fool that he was, but we don't want any villains turning up here, so drink up and let me take over.

"Ta very much and here goes!" He had given her the information and she took his seat and proceeded to stroke the keys with incredible swiftness. *Men of Courage*, Edition limited to 150 copies and our copy *fine*. Price £1000, plus postage and V.A.T.

"Yes, that should do it and if I can finish the rest by eleven and you're a fast driver ... If Pike really was murdered and your hunch is right... Fill in the address of the customer by hand, Mr Mayne, to save me time." She pulled out a card and held it out to him.

"Yes, if you're right somebody will be very angry when he looks at tomorrow's mail."

By nine o'clock of the morning Peggy Tey mentioned, a number of people had read the quotation and dismissed it with sadness, bewilderment or contempt.

His Honour Judge Tenton was on his way to court when he glanced at the card and at first he felt pleasure. He was grateful to Tom for remembering because he was mentioned in the book himself as a former rock climber. Tenton's *Rake on Scafell* and Tenton's *Ruin in the Grampians* testified to his prowess.

Then, his eyes fell on the price and they seemed to draw back in his head and become smaller. Old offenders knew that cold, shrunken look well and many had quailed before it. A hard man, the judge, hard on the bench and hard on the rocks. Not at all a man to fall foul of.

"A fool," he muttered to himself as the car drew up. "A fool or a cheat." He dropped the offending message onto the floor and hurried out to pass a remarkably savage sentence for bigamy.

The Right Reverend Dr Hugo Scanner, Bishop of West Auckland, was slightly more charitable.

"Dear me," he said to his wife and glancing at the card propped up against a coffee-pot. "Old Pike's business has fallen into extremely grasping or ignorant hands it appears. A thousand pounds plus VAT for a book worth twenty." The bishop felt slightly annoyed, though his expression didn't alter. In his youth he had had the misfortune to fall from the yard-arm of a sailing ship and the resulting collision between his face and the deck below had left him with a rigid mask which couldn't really smile or scowl.

"Still one must make allowances, I suppose." He left the breakfast table and crossed to a desk. "Perhaps this man Mayne merely made a typing error ..." He drew a circle in red ink around the price and wrote: "Is this intended as a jest?" Then he signed, "Hugo West Auckland, D.D." with a flourish and slipped the card into an envelope.

"Yes, a Christian priest should always give people the benefit of a doubt," he thought and glanced at a clock. "Still, if the fellow really means what he wrote he is either an imbecile or a knave. A thousand pounds indeed! An insult to his own intelligence and knowledge." Anger rose as he addressed the envelope and considered the enormity of the figure. The Diocesan Conference was due to start in twenty minutes and, though they didn't know it, his assembled clerics were in for a pretty thin time.

But if the judge and the bishop had dismissed the quotation, there were others who did not.

Mr Jason Biggs, Keeper of the Walpole Library, for instance, studied Tom's card carefully and then called for his assistant. "Tell me, Miss Smith," he said, speaking very slowly, as always happened when something disturbed him. "Isn't this the book we had that unpleasantness about?"

"Quite correct, sir. The limited edition of *Men of Courage*, though the serial number is different. Ours was a hundred and one." She had picked up the card and squinted at it through her glasses. "But the price is quite absurd. A thousand pounds! The correct figure should be under thirty as far as I can remember offhand. I know that old Pike always tried to charge the limit, but this man who has taken over his business appears to be . . ."

"A fool or a villain, Miss Smith, though there may be a simple mistake. If Mr Mayne was doing a number of quotations from Pike's stock, he might have mixed it up with another title." As the idea came to him, Biggs's speech speeded up.

"Yes, of course; a simple mistake, but we'd better get onto him at once and ask the proper price. Tell him what happened to our own copy. It might make him more co-operative. A nasty business that, Miss Smith.

"Very objectionable, indeed!"

Less than ten miles away from the Walpole Library Tom's card had hit pay dirt and the book had a potential buyer. Sir Simon Vale, chairman of Allied Chemical Engineering, stared at the quotation and he hardly noticed the price. Once there had been a time when he'd studied every price carefully. Once, there had been a time when he'd haggled over a few shillings, but now he was too old and rich to bother. A thousand was ridiculous of course. This fellow Mayne was a crook, but he wouldn't argue with him. He wanted a copy of *Men of Courage* and here was one for sale.

"I wonder if you'd do me a favour, my dear," he said, smiling at his niece Janet across a vast mahogany table, which was ridiculously large for two people. "Would you run out to Chelsea and pick up a book for me? The man won't find many buyers at his price, but I don't want to lose it."

"Of course I can." Janet smiled back at him and reached for the card. She had lived with Simon Vale since her parents died, several years ago, and they were very fond of each other. They also pitied each other.

Janet pitied her uncle because, though on paper he was still chairman of A.C.E., it was only on paper. Since his last stroke, he had been forced to delegate authority and Peter Kent virtually ran the firm now. Apart from herself, the firm was the one thing that mattered to Sir Simon Vale and he was like a dry husk. An empty shell without hope or interest, but many fears.

On his part, Sir Simon pitied Janet because she was too rich and might someday become too powerful. One of the richest women in England, probably, since he'd transferred that last block of shares to her in the hope of avoiding death duties and keeping the firm in the family. He respected money and power himself. Almost loved them, but without another form of love, they could be very dangerous things.

Wealth – real wealth, not just thousands of pounds, but hundreds of thousands, could make a woman grow sour before her time and he dreaded that that might happen to Janet. A telephone call; the fairy godmother was always available at the end of the line to provide minks and cars, yachts and a string of eager suitors. Also to sow insecurity.

Insecurity, that was the curse of the rich, if they were weak and inexperienced and he'd seen the results a score of times. Women who wore the best clothes and jewellery, women who had the best beauty treatment, who had everything material to live for, sat staring over the blue seas with faces of frightened harlots. Women whose thoughts were always the same. "Does he want me for myself, this time? Is it the real thing at last, or just the cheque-book? Oh, God, if only I was sure he loved me."

"Poor Janet Vale," he thought. She might have to pay for his pride; his stupid, boneheaded ignorance. He'd never encouraged her to take a job or show an interest in the business. Why should his niece have to work when he had money to burn, and how he'd slaved for it.

A woman's place was in the home, that had been his philosophy. There was no reason for Janet to wear her eyes out studying at some damned university. Social work for charity was all right of course, but not for financial gain. Finance was a man's line of country and there was no room at the top for women. Simon Vale had firmly believed that once and now he was beginning to regret his firmness.

"Poor little Janet." The thought kept repeating itself. "Let her marry soon. Let her marry anyone, however old or unattractive he may be. He'll get my blessing providing he has money of his own. Providing he can give her love and some sense of security."

"It's that book, uncle." Janet looked up from the card. "A copy of the one you lost."

"Yes, the book which was lost, stolen or strayed. Most probably borrowed and never returned." Vale gave a tired, sad smile. "Odd thing how perfectly honest people who would always hand over a wallet they found in the street think nothing of borrowing a book and failing to return it." He shook his head wearily. "But in any case, I want that copy. Hubris – personal vanity, maybe, but I figure in one chapter myself."

"I know, Uncle, the *Sam and Helen*." Janet remembered the story well. The *Sam and Helen* was an armoured tugboat which Vale, then a naval lieutenant, had served on during the war. The *Sam* had been sailing back from Murmansk during the end of 1944 when she and her escort were torpedoed and sank within minutes, but her uncle came through. With incredible luck and courage, through ice, fog and mountainous seas, he had brought the survivors home. The lifeboat reached Scotland three weeks later, and there were only four men alive. One of them died later and one was Peter Kent.

"Of course you must have a copy, Uncle, and I won't bother to beat the man down." Janet frowned at Tom's price. "A thousand quid is a bit steep, but it's not every family that can claim to have a hero."

"Thank you, my dear, though collate the book before handing over your cheque. See that the photograph taken from the *Sam*'s lifeboat isn't missing.

"And now I'll get along to the office, Janet. Peter Kent is a good, loyal subordinate. Been with me since the war, but he can't carry the whole concern single-handed!" Vale heaved himself to his feet and walked slowly to the door. Very slowly – since his stroke every step was an effort and Janet knew how much he hated it.

"Goodbye, Uncle," she said, watching those dragging feet on the carpet, which only will-power kept moving. "And don't worry about *Men of Courage*. I'll go round and get Mayne's copy now and have it on your desk by lunch-time. Give me something useful to do for a change." She watched him close the door and grinned to herself. "God knows I need that something."

Forty-five people had received Tom's cards and noted the contents with bewilderment, anger and acceptance. One noted them with sheer murderous rage.

"Number 50." It wasn't the price but the copy number which aroused the man's wrath and he scowled at it over his breakfast. The man believed in large breakfasts and he was large himself. Eighteen stone and all of them bone and muscle. An unpleasant sight, dressed in surprisingly vulgar pyjamas, open at the top to show a mat of reddish hair. He had a flowing ginger moustache and an expression of almost inhuman arrogance. Not at all a man to fall foul of. A very bad enemy at the slightest provocation.

At first, he had merely glanced at the card and then his bulging eyes fell on the number and something rather horrible happened to him. If possible, his body seemed to swell and grow bigger. His tanned, leathery face glowed like a lamp and a string of curses poured from his lips. For a moment he eyed a rhinoceros hide whip on the wall longingly, but soon discarded the idea of using it.

"Too bulky, quite unnecessary," he muttered to himself. "But just wait till I get my hands on you, Mr Thomas Mayne."

Four

Five minutes after Tom opened his shop the next morning, he received a telephone call from the Walpole Library. A long, rambling call with Mr Jason Biggs slurring on the end of the line. But when he finally replaced the receiver, Tom's eyes were very thoughtful. At least, part of his suspicions were true, it seemed. Somebody with an extremely strange and abnormal mind was interested in *Men of Courage*.

He arranged the outside shelves as usual, he read a couple of letters and answered one of them, he paced the floor and thought about Pike's death. He opened the catalogue and studied Pike's list.

It was a lovely day. Spring breaking into summer with the sun peering through the windows and as he looked at the catalogue, his ideas about Pike began to change. He wanted them to change – he wanted to stay alive.

And it could have been suicide, he thought. Even after what Goldsmith and Biggs had told him, Pike had probably killed himself. The fact that a man had an obsession with a certain book didn't make him a murderer and the disappearance of that last copy could be explained. Some dishonest policeman with a taste for literature, slipping it under his coat as he went out.

Yes, he thought, lying to himself and he knew he was lying. The objectionable Mrs Tey was probably right and Inspector Pounder knew his job. After all, he himself was the only person to benefit directly from Pike's death and he'd benefited. The catalogue told him that he was several thousand pounds richer, so why hadn't he stuck to his own business and let the police stick to theirs? If his theory was wrong, those quotations he'd sent would label him a fool or a crook in the eyes of many librarians or collectors. If correct, he'd left himself

42

wide open to a person who had killed once and would have no hesitation in killing a second time.

"Mr Mayne?" He must have closed his eyes for a moment and when he opened them he saw that he had a visitor. One of the most beautiful women he had ever seen was standing before the desk.

"I'm sorry to disturb you, Mr Mayne, but I've come to collect a book you offered my uncle, Sir Simon Vale." Janet smiled and held out a card. She wore a Dior suit and her car parked outside had probably cost more than Tom earned in five years.

"Yes, of course, Miss Vale." Tom had seen that smiling face before in half a dozen social magazines and usually in the company of a sprig of the nobility named the Honourable James Stewart-Smith. "Do please sit down for a moment."

"No need for that." Janet opened her handbag. She saw a man in his late twenties or early thirties; rather pale and shabby, but still attractive. A man who wasn't after her virtue, but only her money, and she laid the cheque before him. "A thousand pounds was the price and I think you'll find that's correct. And don't bother to wrap the book. I'll just check that the pages are all there and take it along with me.

"Miss Vale, give me a minute please." Tom studied her as he spoke. This girl wasn't a murderer or the representative of a murderer, he thought. People like the Vales didn't kill for what they wanted; they didn't need to. They could afford to pay other individuals to do their dirty work.

"I'm afraid I can't accept this because I no longer have the book, but may I ask you a question?" He held the cheque out to her and saw the smile vanish. "Don't think I'm impertinent, but why are you and your uncle prepared to pay such a lot of money for *Men of Courage?*"

"I'm afraid I do find the question impertinent, Mr Mayne." Janet flushed and she looked even better when she was angry. "Rather insolent, in fact. You quoted the book to my uncle and he is prepared to pay what I understand is well over the fair market price. That is all which should concern you, so may I have the book please?"

"Miss Vale." Tom's eyes pleaded with her. "I may have sounded rude and I apologize, but this is very important to me." The plea worked and Janet lowered herself onto a seat. "I know about your uncle by reputation and he's been buying military history for a long time. He may be an extremely rich man, but he's also a collector and collectors are a breed apart. However wealthy they may be, they hate to pay more than what you described as the fair market price. It spoils the fun for them, like cheating at cards when there's no money involved. So why did your uncle accept my quite ridiculous quotation?"

"Yes, I thought it was absurd too." Janet smiled again and relaxed. This man was just an amiable imbecile with too much curiosity. "Till a few years ago my uncle was a very hard business man and he would either have ignored your quotation or beaten you down within minutes. But some time ago he had a stroke and that's left him old and tired and indifferent to small things.

"He wants the book because he features in one chapter; 'The Saga of the *Sam and Helen*'. We used to have a copy of course but it got lost or was stolen."

"Stolen!" Something seemed to explode in Tom's head and he thought of Mr Biggs and leaned forward. "Have you any idea who could have stolen the thing?

"I'm sorry, that is a stupid and impertinent question."

"Mr Mayne – what is the matter?" He turned and saw that Janet was looking at him with concern. "Are you feeling all right?"

"Yes, quite all right, thank you, Miss Vale," he said, but it was a lie. He felt desperately bewildered and lonely and afraid, and one thing he wanted was an ally; someone to talk to.

"Miss Vale, I'm very sorry, but I must confide in you, so please bear with me a little longer. You may be very angry. You may think I'm mad, but I must tell you the truth." He tried to smile and then lowered his head. "You see, I never had the book. Someone took it away."

Tom told his story and when he had finished the girl didn't appear to be angry or believe he was mad. She sat quite still for a moment. Her thoughts seemed to be miles away.

"Well, it seems to me that you're either a fool or a very brave man, Mr Mayne." she said at last. "People do commit suicide, and your friend Pike had a motive. People borrow books and fail to return them, which is probably what happened to our copy. People do many strange things and you could be quite wrong.

"But if you're not wrong and there is an insane collector on the rampage, you could be in trouble. As soon as he got your card he'll know you suspect him and he won't like that.

"He won't like it at all, so why didn't you tell all this to the police and let them handle the matter?

"Yes, I suppose they'd have laughed at you." She had listened to Tom's explanation and nodded. "After all you haven't got much to go on, unless the murderer calls.

"Thanks." She smiled and accepted a cigarette from him. "I'd like to believe you though, Mr Mayne. It would be fun to unravel a mystery."

"Fun!" Tom had a sudden image of the dirk sticking out of Pike's chest. "Miss Vale, you are probably one of the few people who might be able to help.

"You see, if this murderer exists, and I'm not completely insane, we know quite a lot about him now. He had been in contact with Pike for some time, he was a member of or on the staff of the Walpole, he had access to your uncle's library." Tom ticked the points off on his fingers. "Should one person have all those qualifications, we'll be half-way home. If you could check when your uncle's copy was stolen and who might have taken it, I'll attend to the other two problems, Miss Vale."

"And if one name recurs three times, we'll have him, or possibly her."

She inhaled deeply and stood up. "But since we're going to

be partners in crime, please call me Janet, Tom." She held out her hand and took his. Her touch was firm and warm and full of the sort of confidence that money and breeding sometimes produce.

"Good – very good, and now tell me more. I want to know everything you can remember about Pike and his blasted book."

Janet left at ten and Tom had an ally to rely on. They had arranged to meet later and if three names fitted together they would be the name of a murderer.

Business was quiet that morning. Tom served three customers by eleven and one trail proved to be a dead end. Mr Jason Biggs made that quite clear on the telephone. The Walpole's membership was confidential. It was strictly against the rules to reveal any names or addresses and any breach might cost Mr Biggs his job. That was one reason why he had not reported the loss to the police, and the book just wasn't worth the trouble.

No, the thing hadn't been actually stolen, but worse – much worse. Mutilation was the only way to describe what had happened. As he'd said, half the pages had been slashed or torn out, and over twelve of the illustrations were missing, as far as he could remember.

And not just in one chapter or section; that was the disturbing thing. Willy-nilly – quite at random – from start to finish. Personal spite, a vendetta, a feud directed against a book. Unthinkable that such mindless vandalism should have taken place at the Walpole, though there you are. If Mr Mayne would lower his price to thirty pounds, they'd be glad to purchase it, but . . .

No help from Mr Biggs and Tom lowered the phone in frustration, but it rang again almost immediately and he heard a familiar voice, though he couldn't recognize the caller at first.

"Mr Mayne – Tommy Mayne? This is Peggy. Please come over here at once." The words were stammered out as though the speaker was suffering from hay fever. "Peggy Tey at Nor-wood of course. Old Pike's house." The telephone suddenly went dead, and it took Tom less than ten seconds to make a decision. His assistant was due in at noon and the shop could look after itself till she arrived. He had no liking for Mrs Margaret Tey, but if she had news he wanted to hear it. He locked the front door and hurried away towards the car-park.

The weather had started to change for the worse and the traffic was heavy. A cold wind ruffled the Thames as he crossed Chelsea Bridge and the rain started to fall after Brixton. Just a few scattered drops at first, but they soon thickened and he could hardly make out the Crystal Palace spire. A grey, blustery day; it took him almost an hour to reach Norwood, and he had no idea what he would find at journey's end. Mrs Tey might have been ill, or drunk or afflicted by nerves. She might – just might – have had a visitor.

Anything was possible, though it was unlikely that the visitor had called about *Men of Courage*. Tom had crossed out Pike's address and added his own – but – the customer would have contacted him at the shop – but – he would have telephoned for an appointment – but ...

But – again and again the questions ran through his head, but he would know soon. He turned into Pike's road, found a parking place some fifty yards from the house and ran through the rain.

The front door was open, the flat door was ajar, but the room was different and Tom stopped abruptly. Not because of Mrs Tey who was sitting slumped at the desk, staring blindly at him through tear-stained eyes. Not because some of the books had been pulled from the shelves and lay scattered on the floor. One bookcase was moving, creeping across the floor towards him, and he stepped out of its way quickly when he saw the mover.

"Ah, so you are here at last, Mr Mayne," the voice said and it didn't sound like a human voice, nor did the speaker look like a normal human being. The figure was vast and ape-like, apart from a bald head and a flowing ginger moustache. He looked as though he weighed about twenty stone and was in the pink of condition. He smiled and the smile was one of the most unpleasant things Tom had ever seen.

"Taken your time getting here, so let's have a squint at you." He reached out and tilted an Anglepoise lamp at Tom's face. "No, not a thief or a murderer, I think. Not enough guts to break in and steal anything. Merely a receiver of stolen property, or a poor dupe who had it foisted on him in ignorance." The rasping arrogance of the voice seemed to shake the very foundations of the house.

"Well, where is it, man? Providing no damage has been done I might – just might – decide to be lenient."

"I don't know what you're talking about or who the hell you are." Tom struggled to conceal hysteria. "I own this flat and Mrs Tey asked me to come over at once, so please explain yourself."

"*You* want an explanation from *me!*" A dark, angry flush spread across the man's features and he clenched his fists.

"You don't know what I'm talking about, so let me remind you." He nodded at one of Tom's quotation cards lying on the desk. "Are you denying that you sent that?"

"No." Tom tried to remember some of the names on Pike's list, but apart from Simon Vale and Mr Biggs, his mind had become blank. "I sent out several of those quotations, but—"

"Did you, indeed, Mr Mayne?" he was asked. "You used your own address, but Pike's was still legible, so I called here." The intruder eyed Peggy with deep contempt. "Mrs Tey and I are old acquaintances. She has had her dirty fingers in my pocket before, but not this time, my dear. The boot's on the other foot now, and I want the full truth from your friend Mayne.

"You aren't a thief, Mayne, but merely the receiver of stolen goods. The book came into your possession somehow and when you saw the plate you realized its value. A thousand pounds is an extravagant sum to ask for a normal copy of *Courage*, but not for that particular copy: Number 50." His right fist crashed on the desk to emphasize the number.

"So you sat down, Mr Mayne, and wrote quotations to people who might realize its worth, but you slipped up and made a bad mistake. Your little, mean mind ran through a list of names and you typed them out automatically and without thinking. And one of those names happened to be mine, so you're up the creek and in the soup, my friend.

"Now, where is the book? If you've already sold it, things will go very hard on you, Thomas Mayne."

"I haven't sold it, but what about the book plate? Why should that plate make the copy so valuable?" Tom was convinced he was dealing with an insane gorilla, but he wasn't afraid any more; only interested. This was the second person who considered a thousand pounds might be a reasonable price.

"What about the plate?" The effect of Tom's question was extraordinary. A noise which was part curse and part groan burst from the man's lips, his face glowed like a lamp bulb and for a moment he seemed in danger of a heart attack.

"Mr Mayne," he said when at last the power of speech returned. "Don't provoke me for your own sake. I am not a man who suffers fools or insults gladly.

"You must have known as well as I do what is so special about that copy or you would never have offered it at such a figure. All the edition bears facsimile signatures of individuals mentioned in the text. Hilary, Scott, Simon Vale and so forth, but Number 50 bears my personal inscription.

"No, I do not think £1,000 is too much to pay for a book associated with J. Molden-Mott."

"Molden-Mott." As he heard the name a row of bright book jackets slid before Tom's eyes, and he knew who the gorilla was. The books all bore the imprint of a sound publishing house and their format only varied in minor particulars. On each cover the man stood against a jungle, desert or mountain ous background with groups of natives clustered at his side. He wore shorts and sun-helmets, anoraks and climbing boots and there was usually a rope or a rifle slung over his shoulder. The titles were equally in keeping.

With Mott across the Lost Kalahari, Mott's Voyage up the Selva, On the Track of the Yeti, by J. Molden-Mott, to name just three. Yes, Tom had heard about Mr Mott all right. Charlatan, adventurer, author and by all accounts a very dangerous individual indeed.

"It was your copy and somebody stole it?"

"Most certainly, somebody stole it, Mr Mayne, and that somebody will pay for his folly." He glowered at Peggy Tey who had given a deep sob and unclenched his fists. "Six – seven months ago, while I was leading that Arctic expedition you must have heard about some sneak-thief broke into my flat and removed the book. The fellow was obviously a moron, because that was all he did take. A little more knowledge and enterprise and he could have got hold of my notes and diaries; quite priceless stuff.

"All the same, Mr Mayne. Though the loss is comparatively trivial, I want that book back and I want to find the thief. Nobody will rob J. Molden-Mott with impunity." He twisted his hands together as though the felon's neck was already lodged between them. "Well, I'm waiting, my boy, so out with it. Who stole the book – whom did you buy it from?"

Tom didn't answer for a moment. This was the fourth copy he really knew anything about. One had been mutilated, three had been stolen and at least one man had died because of them. Already he was beginning to reject the idea of a maniac – a crazy collector. There was a cold-blooded planning about the business which didn't fit in with lunacy.

"Mr Mott," he said at last. "I think it's time I did put my cards on the table and told you the truth." He stared up at the glowering face above him and nodded. "I never had a copy of *Men of Courage*. I quoted Number 50 at random and I need your help.

"Help, to bring a killer into the open."

"Yes, I'll help you, Mayne, and there are three possibilities." Mott's forehead wrinkled as he considered what Tom had told him. "The mad collector idea, which I don't dismiss entirely, but do not set much store by either. The theory that there is something hidden in one copy which the murderer must get his hands on. The idea that the whole edition contains information which is either incriminating or of great value.

"And you make yourself useful, woman." He paused and snapped his fingers at Peggy Tey. "Thinking is thirsty work, so go and get us a drink; whisky if there is any." He watched her lumber away and scowled. "Bloody woman! Used to live with a crook called Bill Easter, but he had the sense to make off and leave her. About the only sensible thing he ever did do, though that's neither here nor there.

"Interesting that old Simon Vale should have had his copy stolen, however. They keep an army of loyal retainers in that house and it would be difficult to make off with a matchstick.

"I'm not surprised that Simon wants to replace the book though. He and some of his pals had a whole chapter devoted to their exploits and it makes dramatic reading." Tom noticed a tinge of jealousy in Mott's tone. *The Sam and something or other.* A miserable little tug torpedoed off the North Cape at the end of '44. High seas, terrible conditions, but the gallant lieutenant brought the survivors home in a lifeboat.

"Got him a lot of publicity. Probably got him the backers to start his business too. Don't know about that, but I do know that it's a damn prosperous business. If you cut a dash with little Miss Janet, you'll have nothing to worry about, old boy."

"Maybe, but there's not much possibility of that." Tom turned away from the leering face and saw Peggy return with a tray. "And just what do you suggest our plan of action should be?" He both resented Mott and welcomed his cooperation.

"*Our* plan does not exist, Mayne." Mott crossed to the tray and poured himself a glass of neat scotch. "Up to now you have behaved in a most foolhardy and stupid manner, and it's what I say that goes in future. By all means try to find if there's a connection between the Vale household and the Walpole Library, but I doubt if you'll get any joy. Our bird will have covered his tracks too well for that.

"Cheers." He raised the glass and drained its contents in a single manly gulp. "And in a sense, your unpleasant pal Goldsmith could be right. Pike might have found a crazy customer, but what drove the man crazy? Was there something in the book which terrified him? Did he kill Pike because of blackmail?"

"Blackmail! Sorry, I'm not with you!"

"No, I suppose not. You're still struggling to be loyal to your late benefactor, but we must face facts." Mott sounded like a schoolmaster explaining a simple point to a very dense pupil. "Friend Pike is instructed to dig up any copies of *Men of Courage* he can find. Well, after a time he becomes suspicious. He starts to believe that he may not merely have a hoarder on his list of customers, but something far more interesting. Somebody who wants those books not merely to keep and gloat over, but to destroy. Somebody who is frightened because, hidden away in the pages of that book, is a piece of information which can hurt him."

He pulled out a short, blackened pipe and proceeded to ram tobacco into the bowl.

"I met old Pike once or twice in the way of business and I can imagine exactly what he'd do if he suspected anything like that. He'd search through his next copy of the book very carefully and if he found something discreditable, the idea of blackmail would soon enter his squalid mind. No, no, Mayne, don't interrupt me when I'm thinking." He paused and lit his pipe. "I know what you are trying to say. The book was published in 1958, so what possible threat can it contain now?" The pipe was drawing to Mott's satisfaction and grey smoke drifted to the ceiling and slowly dispersed. "Well, the sins of the father, perhaps. Who can have a guilty secret tucked away in a book which was issued so long ago? I don't know yet, but if a man like Pike could stumble on the answer, it shouldn't be difficult for someone like – like – " Modesty prevented him from saying "myself", so he compromised with "somebody of real intelligence, to dig out the truth.

"Yes, my first job will be to get hold of that book and read it very carefully. You, Peggy dear, will see that this flat is kept securely locked and allow nobody to enter – nobody at all.

"You, Mr Mayne, will meet me at your shop this evening, providing you're still alive, which seems unlikely." He poured out more whisky and grinned unpleasantly. "Oh, I mean that, my boy. 'By the pricking of my thumbs something wicked this way comes.'

"Something very wicked, Tommy Mayne, so look after yourself." His great, gnarled fist raised the glass ceremoniously. "If our murderer exists, he will be a man of resource, guile and courage. If you sent him one of those cards, he will be a very angry man. If he received the card … Need I say more?" He emptied the glass and slammed it down on the tray. "No, I think we can safely expect an attack on your life during the next few hours."

The man with the crippled hand was thinking about hell, though not about hell-fire. In his own mind heat had nothing to do with the place of damnation. Fire was a punishment, but it destroyed and gave rest, whilst cold, bitter icy cold; that was the real torment. A wind that numbed the brain and slowed the blood and ended in frost-bite. The skin stripped from the face, the limbs growing black through lack of circulation. An anguish akin to that of a man drowning in biting chemicals. Finally gangrene, and the only cure a knife or a scalpel.

Amputation, but there had obviously been nobody available to operate on Allan's tortured arms and legs. The man looked at the picture of a boy on his table. Allan had probably taken a long time to die, and it had taken him many years to discover who killed him. A labour of love – a labour in vain up to now, because he couldn't prove anything.

Not yet – not just at the moment, but when he had the proof. The man closed his eyes and muttered aloud. " 'Vengeance is Mine,' saith the Lord."

Five

Robert Boyle House, the Headquarters of A.C.E., was a tall, grim building off Holborn Broadway. Here, none of the frills associated with big business were in evidence. Where his factories were concerned, Simon Vale spent money lavishly, but not on the office. "Handsome is as handsome does" was the company motto and any unnecessary show of ostentation raised his instant displeasure.

"I'm sorry, Miss Janet, but Sir Simon is engaged at the moment. A meeting with our American sales manager and . . ." Her uncle's secretary frowned. She had an old, wrinkled face and, like many of the staff, had been with the firm for years. "You know, I shouldn't be saying this, but I do wish he wouldn't come in so often. We all love to see him, of course, but since his stroke, it does seem dangerous. Unnecessary too, as I pointed out to Mr Kent only yesterday."

"Rubbish, Mary. Simon Vale built this concern from nothing, and his presence is all-important." The man had come almost silently into the room and smiled at them. An elderly, stoutish man, but there was nothing weak or flabby about him. He wore his dark suit like a uniform, his face was tanned and his eyes twinkled. "Hello, Miss Janet," he said. "Please don't pay any attention to Mary. She fusses over your uncle like a doting granny, but it's quite all right. The chief may have had an illness but business is the best tonic. I know – we've been together a long, long time.

"Now, come and wait in my room for a moment. I don't think the chief should be long, but we're having trouble with the Laximed sales and that fellow Sinclair is having a strip torn off his back." Peter Kent opened the door and led her across to his own office. A bare, plain room with a steel desk, two filing cabinets and three stiff, hard-backed chairs.

"Do sit down and make yourself comfortable, Miss Janet. A cigarette?" The case on the desk was brass and seemed quite unfitted to a man who was almost the controlling brain in the organization. "By the way, didn't I see your picture in the *Tatler*, not long ago? At Ascot, with some chap with an extraordinary name – Stewart-Smythe, who plays polo."

"You might have done, Peter." She accepted his light and lowered herself onto one of the spartan chairs. "You don't approve of my friends, do you?"

"Not really, I'm afraid, though its none of my business, Miss Janet. I think you could do better however."

"Really, Peter; how very generous of you, but tell me something. Why do you always call me *Miss* Janet? After all, I've known you since I was a child and you're on the board now. Probably the only one that really matters since Uncle became ill. *Miss* makes me feel like a barmaid."

"I'm sorry, Miss Janet. I'd hate to make you feel that, but I just can't think of you in any other way, just as Sir Simon will always be the skipper or the chief to me. You see almost my whole life has been spent working for one man and I'm too old to alter now."

"I know that, Peter. You and Uncle were on the *Sam* together, but the war's been over a long time, and surely you can accept me as an equal?"

"The *Sam* – the old *Sam and Helen*." He nodded at a photograph on the wall. "She's the point, I'm afraid. The reason why we can never be equals." He crossed to the picture and his fingers stroked the glass. "Not much to look at, is she? Just an ocean-going salvage tug of under a thousand tons displacement and built on the Tyne in 1938. Taken over by the navy when the war started and fitted out as a rescue ship." Peter Kent was speaking partly to himself. "My first vessel as a petty officer and Sir Simon's first as a lieutenant.

"Northern Russia was our destination, and we only just scraped through. Crew of *twenty-five* when the *Sam* started out from Loch Ewe, but ten of them bought it before we reached Kola Inlet. Two swept overboard by heavy seas and eight machine-gunned from the air. Another three were put ashore at Murmansk. They either vanished or died in hospital. I don't know, but there was no shore leave for the rest of us.

"No booze either. We just rotted off that dead wilderness and watched the convoys come and go."

"The old, old story, eh, Peter?" The door was open, and Kent had been overheard. Another man came into the room, limping slightly and grinning at Janet. "Good-day, miss," he said. "Back to the North Cape again – the *Sam and Helen*."

"Well, don't let Peter bore you too much. I, Willie Mackenzie, was on that damn tug too and I left three toes in her."

"I know that, Willie, but I'm not bored." Janet watched William Mackenzie grimace as he sat down. Another war-time companion and another right-hand man, chief chemist of A.C.E. and almost as important as Kent for the firm's survival. "I've always wanted to hear the full story, but my uncle hardly ever talks about it."

"Why should he? Sir Simon is a modest man and would not blow his own trumpet." Mackenzie's Scottish accent became more pronounced. "Go on and finish your tale, Peter. I'll no interrupt youse."

"You'd best not, Willie." Kent cleared his throat and continued. "Well, as I said, we waited, miss. For eleven and a half months we rotted at Murmansk and then the orders came and the *River Madoc* put in.

"One of the new River Class frigates and she'd been sent to escort us home. One warship for a single little tugboat. Seemed ridiculous, but we weren't told why and we never asked. We were just too pleased to have her protection."

"And we did." Mackenzie had forgotten his promise not to interrupt. "With only half our normal crew we kept in the *Madoc's* wake. Out of the Inlet and south of Bear Island. I was the second engineer and working watch and watch; four hours on and four hours off. Damn near fell asleep over the diesels, and then just after the North Cape came the first torpedo.

"Never saw it down in the engine-room, of course, but I heard the explosion and I felt the second. Caught us in the stern it did and knocked me unconscious. Peter here dragged me out and, when I came round, the *Madoc* had bought it and we wus sinkin'.

"Every man for himself it was, but the chief, your uncle, stopped any rush for the boats. 'We will leave this vessel in an orderly manner, lads,' he said on the loudhailer, and we did, though we left half a dozen dead behind.

"The old *Sam* went down a few minutes later and the chief took a photograph of her from the lifeboat. You could see the *Madoc's* bow still visible on the horizon." He paused at the memory for a second and then continued.

"We searched for survivors of course, but it was a labour in vain, because the fog closed in and we were alone. Alone off the North Cape, in December, with the cold.

"And God, it was cold, miss. Cold I hope you will never experience and frostbite put paid to me left foot afterwards. Seven men in a lifeboat with only the bergs and flows for company, and the chief.

"Yes, the chief brought us home, Miss Janet. He had the sail hoisted. He did the navigation. He kept us going. 'You've only three things to worry about, lads,' he said. 'The cold and the fog and *me*.'

"Fierce he was. Callous, one might say, but he had to be, and it paid off. Four men reached Scotland, though it took 'em twenty-two days; Peter here, Ernie Sykes, me and the chief . . ."

"Taking my name in vain, Willie?" Sir Simon Vale had appeared in the doorway, standing very straight and erect for a man who had recently recovered from a severe stroke. As Peter Kent had said, business seemed to be his best tonic. "You are in good company, Janet. Peter and William and I are the only members of the firm who matter since poor Ernie Sykes died, and have you got it?"

"It?" Janet took a moment to realize what he was talking

about and then she remembered. "No, I'm sorry, Uncle. The book wasn't available."

"Not available, Jan, but I don't understand. What happened, my dear? Surely the man couldn't have sold it so soon."

"No, he didn't sell it, Uncle, but are you feeling all right?" Janet saw his eyes flicker and he clutched the door post for support.

"Of course I'm all right, girl, but what became of the book? I only received his offer this morning, so the man must still have it or sold the copy elsewhere."

"It's not as simple as that, Uncle." Janet had promised to keep Tom's theory a secret, but concern for Vale made the promise seem unimportant now. Since her own parents had died in a motor crash twenty years ago he was the only family she had, and he looked tired and ill – and forlorn. "You see a copy of *Men of Courage* was bought by a man named Pike at an auction. He paid well over the odds for it and then died. Tom Mayne inherited his stock and . . ."

"I know that, Janet." Sir Simon gave a quick nervous shake of his head. "The card was headed 'successor to', but what became of the book?"

"We don't know, Uncle, but Pike's copy vanished. It disappeared about the time he was killed and Tom Mayne thinks that *Men of Courage* had something to do with his death. He sent out a lot of phoney cards to try to bring a thief into the open."

"A thief! Sorry, my dear, but I don't understand you." Vale's face looked quite empty and stripped of character; the face of a child who has just lost a much-loved toy.

"I'll try to explain, Uncle. You see, during the last few months Pike had been buying copies of that book and somebody has probably been stealing them as well. One in a library was mutilated and Tom Mayne believes that a mad collector could be at work. A lunatic with a pathological obsession for . . . Uncle, what is the matter?"

"A lunatic." A single, sharp laugh burst from Vane's lips and he staggered forwards. "So that's what Mr Mayne thinks – just a lunatic.

"Your friend seems to be a smart fellow, my dear, but he's wrong, you know, horribly wrong ..." His eyes were wide open and looked as though they were staring at the gates of hell.

"Just a lunatic, Janet. Oh, if only Mr Mayne was right, my dear." The eyes closed, his knees buckled and he slid into the arms of Peter Kent.

Six

Sir Simon Vale had had a second stroke and been borne unconscious to his bed. Janet had listened to the doctors and knew that this time it might be the end. Tom Mayne had spent a fruitless day searching for copies of *Men of Courage*. Mr Mott had been engaged on a similar project.

The Raeburn Press had ceased to exist as an independent concern years ago, but they still did business as a branch of Porter and Triggs who occasionally issued an expensively got-up edition under their imprint. Within one hour of Tom Mayne's leaving him, Mott marched into Porter House, grinned at the receptionist and announced, "Mott for Levin," in loud, booming tones.

"Have you an appointment, sir?" The girl studied the visitor and decided that he had not. She also fancied she could distinguish the sheep from the goats and Mott was clearly a goat. The author of some worthless, trashy manuscript bent on bothering the directors and she repeated the question and smiled maliciously. "An appointment, sir."

"Of course I haven't made an appointment, but my name is Mr J. Molden-Mott and I wish to see Judas Levin immediately.

"That means at once, girl, so get through to him on the blower and be quick about it."

"As you wish, sir." She was still smiling as she lifted the house telephone and dialled a number. In a moment she would be told to send this objectionable caller about his business. She delivered his message and then gasped. Mr Judas Levin had appeared in person with his hand outstretched and he beamed at Mott like an Israelite viewing the Promised Land for the first time.

"Mr Molden-Mott, this is a pleasure." Judas Levin didn't actually kiss Mott, but he still smiled as his hand was crushed

in a vice-like grip. "How kind of you to call and see us. Such
a friendly gesture and let's go into my office and have a real
man-to-man natter." He led the way to a door on the left and
nodded at his secretary who was holding it open. "Some tea,
Betty, and please hurry. My guest is a very busy man." Levin
had met Mott on several occasions and knew a great deal
about him; little of it good. The fellow was a boor and a brag-
gart and a very objectionable person indeed. All the same, his
books sold well; there was no denying that. Twenty thousand
in hardcover alone, not to mention the paper and serial rights.
Porter and Triggs had had a rough time recently and Mott
could be a welcome tonic to their list.

"That's right. Do sit down and make yourself comfortable,
sir." He watched Mott lower his bulk into his own chair behind
the desk and leaned back against the mantelpiece. "Very
strange that you should call today of all days, Mr Mott. I just
finished reading *The Track of the Snowman* last night and found
it fascinating." The lie came fluently and easily. "Remarkably
interesting and your publishers would be quite safe in offering
a reward for anyone who could put it down unfinished." Levin
had high hopes regarding Mott's visit and wanted to turn
the conversation onto the right channels. "Sales going well, I
hope. Twenty to twenty-five thousand?"

"The title of the book is the *Yeti*, Mr Levin, and sales are
not all right." Mott reached out for his host's cigar case and
sniffed a Double Corona. "Not right at all. Only twenty-eight
according to Rexten's last accounts which is highly unsatisfactory.

"Got a match on you?" He had snipped the end of the cigar
and waited for Levin to produce a slim gold lighter. "Thanks.

"Though I say it myself and I'm the most modest man
alive, that book is by far the best thing that's been done on the
subject and twenty-eight thousand is chicken-feed. When I
think of the numbers Collins sold, about that wretched lion-
ess and compare her to my Yeti . . ." He broke off and pulled
at the cigar. "Advertising, or rather the lack of it, is the real

trouble of course. If that ass, George Bulljohn, had had any sense of proportion, he'd have splashed my picture across every newspaper and magazine in the country." He broke off again and considered Mr Bulljohn and the sufferings of other literary figures. Dean Swift exhibited as a freak to the Dublin mob; Chatterton starving in his attic; Shakespeare ... He was almost certain that Shakespeare had been betrayed at some point, but he couldn't remember by whom.

"Quite so." Levin beamed sympathetically. The conversation was going exactly as he hoped. "Rexton used to be a most respectable firm, but since old Peter Rexton retired, they seem to lack vision.

"It is not for me to criticize a rival of course, but if we had someone like yourself on our list; someone whose books would really sell given the right treatment; no trouble or expense would be too much to offer."

"They'd sell all right, given proper advertisement and publicity." Mott had disliked Judas Levin for some time, but now he seemed to be a remarkably civil fellow, and intelligent too, once you got to know him.

"I'm sure that's true, Mr Mott, and if you ever think of a change, do bear us in mind." Levin pressed his advantage. "I'm sure you'd find our production satisfactory and we do have a go at publicity. Also, we'd be proud to have you with us."

"I'm sure you would, old boy." Mott laughed loudly and scornfully. "Not only proud, but overjoyed, I should say. Which publisher would not? Why, if I decided to give Rexton and Bulljohn the heave ho, there'd be a queue of you fellows waiting outside my door, cap in hand.

"Yes, I might consider your firm if I decided on a change, though there's little chance of that at the moment. Bulljohn has a verbal option on my next two works and as you know, an Englishman's word is his bond.

"Ah, and here comes your good lady with our refreshment." He looked up as Levin's secretary laid a tray on the desk. "The cup which cheers, but does not inebriate; worst luck."

"Thank you, Betty." There was a slight coldness in Levin's tone now. He had resented the phrase "cap in hand". He disliked the reference to Englishmen keeping their bonds. Since his hopes of transferring Mott's allegiance from Rexton had faded, he was beginning to regret his hospitality.

"And now, Mr Mott, though I wouldn't describe myself as being overworked, I have things to do, so just what did you want to see me about?"

"Ah, of course. Completely slipped my mind for a moment." Mott poured out tea, added milk and sugar and raised the cup ceremoniously. "Cheers, Mr Levin, and here's to *Men of Courage*, bless their little hearts."

"To what?" Judas Levin was 58, but he suddenly looked much older than his years. "The Death Book? What about it, Mr Mott?"

"Are you hard of hearing, Mr Levin? I never mentioned the *Tibetan Book of the Dead*." Mott scowled at him. "My interest is in a volume entitled *Men of Courage* published by the Raeburn Press during 1958; the year you took them over."

"I know. I heard you all right and please forgive me." Levin's hand was shaking too badly for him to fill his own cup. "I'm rather superstitious, you see, and I used that title ill-advisedly. A sort of personal foible, but why, Mr Mott? Why should *Men of Courage* interest you?"

"Nothing very exciting, I'm afraid." Mott lied fluently though he had noticed Levin's distress and found the name "Death Book" extremely appropriate. "It's just that I'm considering a series of articles to debunk those 'men of courage'; Roland Rawson in particular. I believe he's mentioned in the text, and need the book as a reference to expose his boasts. But it is pretty hard to come by these days, and I hoped you could help me."

"Extremely hard." A little nervous tic was trembling beneath Levin's left eye. "I'd only just started here when we bought out Raeburn and their stock was part of the deal; the 'Death Book' included. Sorry, *Men of Courage*, I should say, and it was only in the proof stage then." He stared at the grey smoke drifting from Mott's cigar.

"A difficult book to market as you can imagine. Too general for one thing and each chapter had been written by a different author; most of them unknown. We didn't know what to do with the wretched thing for some time and then ..." He paused and dabbed his face with a handkerchief. "Mr Triggs, our senior editor in those days, was a bit of a gambler and he decided to take a chance. A limited edition of a hundred and fifty copies were offered to people mentioned in the text and to other individuals who might be interested. All we kept was one set of proofs on file."

"Which has since vanished or been destroyed." There was no surprise in Mott's tone. He somehow knew that this enterprising collector must have paid the publisher a visit. "What exactly happened to your copy, Mr Levin?"

"I'll tell you the little I know, Mr Mott, though it really is very little." Levin tucked away his handkerchief, but the tic still trembled under his eye. "Yes, *Men of Courage*, the *Death Book*," he said. "A strange story, but some time ago, just before last Christmas, we had an enquiry from a dealer asking whether we had a copy available. I'm afraid I can't remember his name, but my secretary might have kept his letter somewhere."

"The name was Pike?"

"Yes, that's right, Mr Mott. John or James Pike, I think it was. He said he had a customer who, like yourself, wanted the book for research and would pay well for a clean copy. I wrote back and told him that, though the edition had been out of print for years, there was a set of files available and his client was welcome to consult them on the premises. It's always been the firm's policy to preserve a copy of everything we've published; mainly for legal reasons.

"Anyway, that was the last we heard from Pike, and I presumed he'd found a copy elsewhere. I didn't give him or *Men of Courage* a thought till our annual stocktaking was made last month."

"And your proofs were missing?"

"Yes, Mr Mott, but I've never been able to understand why. Who would wish to steal such a thing?" Levin's false teeth made a sharp clicking sound. "What possible motive could there be?"

"The question is, who had the opportunity, old boy?"

"Well, only Paul Mason, our filing clerk and general dogs-body had a key to the basement as far as I know. The files are all kept down there and if anyone needed to consult a set, they'd have to get written permission from myself or one of the other directors and Paul would open up for them. But why, Mr Mott? Why should old Paul Mason have taken the proofs? The book had no real value, and Paul had been with the firm for years. Since he was a boy in fact and I'd have trusted him with my last penny."

"Perhaps you would have done, Mr Levin, but what do we really know about other human beings?" Mott imagined what might have happened. Pike's customer had asked him to check with the publishers and Pike had telephoned or written back to say that, though there was no copy for sale, they had one on file. It would have been fairly easy for that versatile client to discover who had charge of the files.

"Could I have a word with this chap Mason, Mr Levin?" he asked.

"A word – with Paul Mason." Levin's teeth rattled again. "No, that's quite impossible, Mr Mott. Mason's not with us any more, and though I didn't suspect there was any connec-tion between him and the loss of that book, I wonder – just wonder if his death had anything to do with it."

"You mean . . ."

"I mean nothing, Mr Mott, but I was at the inquest and there was no doubt at all. Seven days after I replied to Pike's letter, old Paul Mason killed himself."

At least two people had died because of the book and Mr Molden-Mott hadn't enjoyed himself so much for years.

He swaggered up the steps of the British Museum, and the thought that he should have reported what he knew to the police never occurred to him. Why should it? His ability and brains were far superior to anything the rozzers could offer and he had a personal score to settle. Somehow, this sneak-thief, this cold-blooded murderer, had discovered that he owned a copy, and had broken into his flat and stolen it while he was away. In Mott's view, revenge seemed a most worthy motive for tracking the villain down, and to hell with the law.

And he could imagine exactly what had happened at the publishers. The contemptible Judas Levin might say, "Old Paul Mason had been with the firm for years, would have trusted him with my last penny," but he had also used the term "general dogsbody" and mentioned what the dogsbody was paid. Just enough to keep Mason and his invalid wife from starvation and the dog might have heard the whistle of another master and responded.

Yes, poor old Mason might have accepted a bribe to borrow an unimportant book which wouldn't be missed till the annual stocktaking, and he had died accordingly. That murder had been a nasty, unnecessary crime and a nasty, unwholesome brain had done the planning.

Mott pushed through the doors of the Reading Room, checked his reference and handed the slip to an attendant. On paper, at least, the BM had a copy of *Men of Courage*. He just hoped that someone else hadn't got to it first.

"Nothing but blackamoors, Indians and RC priests seem to use the room these days." He sat down and stared scornfully at the collection of woolly heads, turbans and clerical collars bent over volumes. On his right, two clergymen were busily at work; one learning his office, the other studying Ruff's *Guide to the Turf*.

"A nasty, vile crime," he thought. "Pike's death had been quite different, because he was a sharp, grasping man and probably a blackmailer to boot. But Mason – no. There'd been no need to kill Paul Mason.

"I'm engaged in a bit of research, Mr Mason, and you might be able to help me." Mott imagined the first innocent approach made in a café, a bus or a tube train. "You have the key to your firm's filing section, and there's a book that I need to borrow for a few days.

"Be prepared to pay you a hundred for the service and I hope you consider the offer satisfactory."

Yes, a hundred quid would be about right. Not enough to arouse suspicion, but a very pleasant temptation for a poor man, and Mason had accepted the bribe, and wrapped up the proofs next day. He'd strolled along the Thames embankment with the parcel under his arm, and he might have spoken to his benefactor before handing it over.

"You'll not tell anyone about this, will you, sir? I've never been in any trouble before, and . . ."

"You won't be now, Mr Mason, and don't worry at all. Nobody will ever know the reason for our transaction. Not even you, Mr Mason." A hand had reached out for the parcel and another hand came up. Mason's thin, old body had twisted over the parapet and into the Thames water and mud. On the embankment someone had walked away past Cleopatra's Needle and the sphinxes had gone on smiling.

Fair enough, but why? Why kill the poor bastard, when there was no need? Why not just remain anonymous, pay the money, borrow the book and fail to return it? And what was so important about a set of proofs printed almost thirty years ago to provide a motive for at least two murders? Mott's blackmail theory had started to fade and he almost started to accept Tom's notion that a crazed collector might be at work.

All the same, why and what? What attraction could *Men of Courage* contain to drive even a lunatic to murder? Well, in a few minutes, he should find out. It would be very difficult, almost impossible, to steal the BM's copy and in its pages he might learn the truth.

"Why – Why – What?" Quite involuntarily, but loud and clear the words burst from his lips and thundered around the room. The cleric at his side frowned and pointed at the *Silence* notice before returning to his sporting studies. Some very undesirable persons were allowed to use the Reading Room these days, he clearly decided.

"The volume you asked for, sir." The attendant had also heard Mott's outburst and though he whispered, the "sir" sounded vaguely insolent. "I hope you will treat it with care."

"Don't worry about that, my man. Just put the thing down and attend to your other duties." Mott had resented the fellow's tone and normally he would have given him a piece of his mind. At the moment, however, he was just too pleased to see the book intact to feel anger.

He didn't open it at once though, but stared at the cover with something like love in his eyes. The original blue vellum had been replaced by a drab library binding, but the title showed it was what he wanted; the book which was a key to reveal a very sinister murderer. Also a key to fame and fortune and Mott enjoyed praise. Already he imagined the voices of old, authoritative men discussing his triumph in clubs. "Smart fellow, Molden-Mott. Solved the Norwood and Embankment murders single handed. Police thought they were suicides, but Mott knew better. Once, he got his nose to the scent, the business was as good as over. Mott – Mott – Molden-Mott." Like a peal of victory, his own name rang through his head, and then at last, slowly and expectantly, a lover approaching the bed of his beloved, an explorer climbing the last pass into an undiscovered country he opened the cover and looked at the title page.

"*Men of Courage. An account of Human Heroism, covering two Centuries.*" He picked up the book, turned to the first chapter and started to read.

But as he did so, every face in the room swung towards him. Black, brown and white features took on expressions of horror and astonishment, and three attendants came bounding across the floor. For Mott's own face had become a mask of baffled fury, and his cry of anger was scarcely human.

"Oh, you bastard," he shouted at the top of his voice. "You bloody, wicked, clever bastard!"

Between his fingers the pages of the book had crumbled into greyish powder and were drifting away.

Seven

"Acid, the bastard used acid. Three capsules of vitriol at a guess, though I can't be sure about that." Mott scowled at Tom and Janet and his voice was full of injured dignity and humiliation. He remembered the pleasure he had felt on being handed the book, and the excitement on reading the title page. And then there was no more enjoyment and no more print to read. The pages had crumbled into a cloud of grey powder and vanished into thin air.

The sequel was even more hideous. With an attendant on either side he, J. Molden-Mott, had been marched through lines of indignant faces to the curator's office and treated as though he was a juvenile delinquent. "The fellow dared to accuse me of destroying the book, Mayne; me of all people."

"Rather a neat idea, though." In spite of Mott's indignation Tom had to grin, because the idea really was neat. It would have been almost impossible to steal or damage the BM's copy by normal methods, so a novel form of attack had been used. Little capsules of lighter fuel filled with vitriol and strapped in place with adhesive tape. In time, the acid would have eaten through the plastic containers and started to run through the pages. Though he sympathized with Mott's feelings, there was something very comical about the drifting, grey confetti and he was glad to see that Janet shared his view. She was staring at the floor and trying to conceal a smile.

They sat in the back room behind his shop, hemmed in by unsorted books and manuscripts and unframed prints. The shop itself was closed for the night, but through the glass partition he could see that one industrious browser was still browsing. An old though not a very valued customer who could be relied on to steal nothing and let himself out.

"I suppose one might call it neat, in a crazy and objection

able sort of way." Mott had obviously noticed Janet's smile and resented it. "We've got a rum bird on our hands, Miss Vale. When he can buy or steal he does so, if not he mutilates and destroys. If necessary he becomes a completely ruthless murderer.

"Very rum, very dangerous, and he must have got hold of most of the edition by now, though we do not know why he wants the copies, or what they contain. Without that knowledge we're snookered and I gathered you had no luck, old boy."

"No, not even a smell of the damned book." Tom remembered the fruitless hours he had spent on the telephone and the replies which were always the same. "*Men of Courage*, Mayne. Haven't seen one for years, but you might try Elder at Bournemouth."

"Can't help you, Tom. Think I sold one some time ago, but God knows who to. Henry Coverdale might be able to fit you up, though it's doubtful."

"Let me see. No I'm afraid not, but give James Thin of Edinburgh a ring, but it's a hundred to one against."

Always the same. A negative response and advice to try somebody else. A hundred to one, or a thousand to one, the odds seemed hopeless. Tom dreaded the thought of his next phone bill.

"Then our only hope is that the joker panics and makes an attack on you, Mayne. After all, you are Pike's heir and successor." The thought seemed to cheer Mott up and he nodded as there was a knock on the door. "But you have business to attend to, it appears."

"Good-evening, Mr Mayne." The browser entered and approached Tom, creaking like an unoiled gate. He was very tall and thin and extremely old and held out a book as though it was a rather disgusting and germ-ridden object.

"Sorry to bother you so late, Mr Mayne, but I found this and wondered about the price marking. Thirty pounds seems terribly high you know."

"May I see, Major Laker." Tom took the book from him and frowned. "Corvo's *Weird of the Wanderer*. I don't think that thirty is at all too high."

"Not normally, but in this condition." The aged warrior looked slightly offended as though a close friend was trying to swindle him.

"As you can see the spine and covers are rubbed, a flyleaf is missing and there's a lot of foxing everywhere. Foyle's had a much better copy for only twenty, the other day."

"All right, twenty it is." Normally, Tom would have used the obvious retort, "Then why didn't you buy from Foyles?" and held out for the full price, but he just wanted to get rid of Laker. He watched the major lay down the money and creak away out, well pleased with his bargain.

"Business indeed, Mayne." Mott grimaced at the four five-pound notes and winked at Janet. "Do you manage to make a living from this dump, old boy?"

"I survive, thank you." Tom realized that he had never disliked a human being as much as Molden-Mott. It had been very pleasant talking to Janet before Mott arrived and shoul-dered his way through the shop, full of his treatment at the British Museum, what he had learned from Mr Levin, and ogling Janet in a most repellent way.

"Miss Vale. This is a great, great pleasure, and you are far more beautiful than your photographs led me to expect. Quite ravishing, but I was so sorry to hear about your uncle's second stroke, and do hope he will make a speedy recovery.

"What a man he must be! A great captain of industry and a war hero too. Bringing that lifeboat back from the Arctic was one of the finest things I ever read about, and I understand that he still sailed till quite recently."

"Yes, the *Bully Boy* was the name of his yacht, but she hasn't been out since one of his original partners died, Mr Mott."

"Yes, damn Mott and damn Janet too," Tom thought. She really seemed to appreciate the man and blushed at his com-pliments. She appeared grateful for his sympathy and talked about her blasted uncle with pride. "Four of them started the firm as soon as they were demobbed in 1946, Mr Molden-Mott, though I never knew how they managed with such a little capital. Only their gratuities really, but somehow A.C.E. succeeded."

"And genius, dear lady. Never forget that quality. A few – a very few men have it whilst others lack talent." Mott had looked at Tom with contempt.

"But I do hope our young friend Mayne hasn't been boring you before I got here and now I will tell you of my own experiences." He said and Janet listened. She listened humbly and with deep attention to Mott's encounter with Judas Levin. She frowned sadly as she heard of his humiliations at the British Museum; only that slight smile suggested she was amused.

But what did it matter and why should he worry? Tom tried to face the facts. He had as much chance of dating Janet Vale as finding an original papyrus of the Book of Genesis. Girls like Janet scarcely noticed little second-hand booksellers with shops in suburban streets and he suddenly wanted to be rid of the whole affair.

"My business is no concern of yours, Mr Mott," he said. "Except that it concerns one book, which has cost the lives of two people already. We can't get hold of a copy, so isn't it time we did the next best thing and told the police all we know? They'd have to act on the information we gave them."

"Would they – would they indeed, Tommy Mayne?" Mott flushed angrily. "On the whole our rozzers are a hard-working but unimaginative men and what could they discover that – that—" He was about to say "I" but gallantly changed it to "that Miss Vale and myself fail to unearth." He beamed at Janet as though she was a clever and pretty child.

"And now, my dear, though I know how upset you must be by Sir Simon's illness, please try to help me. Was there anyone in your house, a relative, a guest or a servant, who might have taken that book and also had access to the Walpole Library?"

"Nobody that I know of." Janet shook her head. "You see

the book was stolen months ago, and almost anyone could have taken it. I think my uncle is a member of the Walpole, but I don't believe he's been there for years. I'll ask him of course, but the doctor won't allow him to talk freely for a long time." Janet lowered her eyes and suddenly felt guilty. She had said that her uncle had had a stroke, but not what had caused it. Nor what he said when he toppled into the waiting arms of Peter Kent or what his face had looked like. "Just a lunatic, Janet. Oh, if only that were true." She had no idea what the book contained, but she somehow suspected that the Vale family were threatened by it.

"Another customer, old boy. More big business." Major Laker had left, but someone else was pounding on the outside door and Mott hurried to answer it. "You and Miss Vale will stay here, Mayne," he said. "I'll deal with this joker." He opened the door and then gasped.

"You, woman," Tom and Janet heard him roar. "Why are you here? I ordered you to remain near Pike's flat and keep an eye open for any visitors. Why have you disobeyed me and deserted your post, Mrs Tey?"

"Because of the post, Mr Mott, and I ain't deserted anyone; men keep deserting me." Peggy Tey was frightened of Mott and her voice certainly showed it. "These were popped through Mr Pike's letter-box this morning and I thought they might be important."

"They might be, though I doubt it." Mott grabbed four envelopes out of her hand. "Now, back to duty, Peggy Tey. Home to Norwood." He slammed the door in her face and returning muttering. "Great, fat, bloated cow – disobedient, prying bitch.

"I beg your pardon, Miss Vale," he apologized. "But that woman's been my cross for years. An extremely heavy cross to bear." He flung the letters on the desk and glowered at Tom. "Well, open them, man. As you're Pike's heir, I suppose that's your right."

"Thank you." Tom opened the envelopes and the first three

were quite unimportant; a gas bill, a demand for the rates, an enquiry from an American dealer requiring back copies of Jane's *Fighting Ships*. He pushed them aside and picked up the last exhibit.

The envelope was quite ordinary but addressed in a very beautiful hand, probably by someone who regarded penmanship as an art as well as a means of communication. He tore open the flap and pulled out a single sheet of paper with a neatly printed heading. "Honeysuckle Cottage, Wildflower Walk, Ladyburn, Buckinghamshire."

"Dear Mr Pike," Tom read. "As it is now almost a year since we met, I trust you have not forgotten our little transaction of last July.

"If not, you will remember asking me to contact you, should I wish to dispose of any more of my cousin's books. You were especially interested in the second copy of . . ."

"Good grief." Tom broke off and whistled. "Yes, this is important and we've got a break at last. He started to read aloud, but Mott suddenly leaned forward and snatched the letter from him.

"Cor stone the crows." He tilted the paper into the light and chuckled. "Listen to this, Miss Vale.

"The second copy of a book entitled *Men of Courage*, which, as I told you, had been mislaid. This has now materialized, however, and should you still wish to purchase it, I would be glad if you could call and see me. As I am completely confined to the house now, there is no need for you to bother to make an appointment. Yours, very truly – Elsie Marley."

"Hallelujah!" Mott gave a bellow of triumph and broke into a jig, holding the letter in his ape-like hands and singing as he went.

"Elsie Marley's grown so fine,

She won't get up to feed the swine . . ."

A pile of books barred his progress, but he kicked them aside and continued.

"But stays in bed till eight or nine,

Bonnie Elsie Marley.

"Yes, really in luck, dear comrades and friends." He raised the paper to his lips and gave it a smacking kiss. "A copy to get our teeth into at last and find out what Mr X is after." He came to a halt and looked at his watch.

"Six thirty though, and Ladyburn's a good hour's run from here, so we'd better get cracking right away. From her note, Elsie appears to be an elderly lady and a stickler for the proprieties. It won't do to arrive too late or for all of us to go barging in; so, who shall visit her? Fair's fair, Mayne, and I'll toss you for it." He took a fifty-pence piece out of his pocket and grinned at Tom. "You call, dear boy.

"Heads, eh, and tails it is." He spun the coin and thrust it away before Tom could even look at the surface. "Well, all's fair in love and war and let's be off, Miss Vale."

"No, I'd rather wait here, Mr Mott." Janet shook her head. "You shouldn't be more than three hours and we'll see you then."

"Really – how extraordinary." Mott looked slightly put out. "Well, there's no accounting for tastes, but I would have thought ..." He shrugged, reached for his hat and then stopped dead. "No, we haven't been thinking, have we? Not about the prime mover – the man who bought the books. Mr J.R. Price designed an aircraft and it crashed and killed and injured a large number of people. Faulty design was the cause, and the scandal made Mr Price change his name, shave off his beard and assume another occupation.

"Mr Price is as good as dead, so Mr Pike takes over. Can't you see what I'm talking about, Mayne?" He frowned at Tom's expression. "Did Pike buy copies of *Men of Courage* to sell 'em, or for a very different reason? Did a victim of that air crash have a friend or a family, who might wish to avenge him? Does the book contain an account of the accident and a picture of the relatives? If so Mr Jonathan Pike had a very good reason to buy up all the existing copies he could lay his hands on, and destroy 'em.

"Self-preservation! The best motive I know, but a pity that it failed, and somebody got to Pike first. Maybe not a friend or a relative, but a survivor. Some one who was horribly crippled in the crash and craved for personal vengeance." Mott clearly relished the thought and he grinned. "Yes, a cripple, I like that. A horrible mutilated and scarred figure might have rung Pike's bell and stuck his dirk through the blighter.

"Well, chattering away here won't solve the problem and I'll be on my way. Providing Miss Marley's copy has a chapter on the K. 107, we'll be half-way home and dry. If you wish to hang about in this dump, Miss Vale, that's your own affair, but give me a ring at my flat any time after ten." He tossed a visiting card onto the desk and strode purposefully out.

"You loathe him, don't you?" Janet reached out and fondled Tom's hand. "You'd like to cut him into little pieces and . . ."

"And flush him down the drain; together with his deformed murderer. Yes, I certainly would." She had so accurately echoed his thoughts that Tom smiled back. "I don't know anybody who gets on my nerves like Mr bloody Mott. If I wasn't sure he could tear me apart with one arm tied behind his back, I'd deliver a punch on his bulbous nose."

"Poor Tom." He caught a trace of her very expensive perfume. "Yes, Mott is a most trying individual, and I'm sure he cheated you over that coin. All the same, he's on his way to Ladyburn now, so what about buying me a drink and a snack."

"I'd like to very much." Tom paused and grinned at her. "But do you think I can afford it?"

"What?" They were still in the shop and Janet glanced around the shelves. "Oh, Mott's comment on making a living still rankles. I'd say you can afford it, Tom. You've got a pretty good stock at the moment."

"Thanks, but do you know much about the second-hand book trade, Miss Janet?"

"*Miss* Janet. Please don't call me *Miss*." She frowned and let go his hand. "You make me feel like Peter Kent does. He's my uncle's managing director now and a very rich man. I've known Peter for years. We should be close friends, but he always calls me Miss Janet, like a servant.

"No. I don't know much about the book trade, Tom, but I can recognize good books." She changed the subject abruptly, as Tom switched off the lights. "Thanks," Janet smiled as he held the door open for her and then nodded through the side window. Its lower half was almost filled by a Hogarth folio opened at the centre plate of the *Harlot's Progress*. "But that poor girl's been there too long and she's becoming faded."

"Faded and foxed and fly-blown, I know. Had an anonymous note about her, stuffed through the letter-box, last week." Tom shut the door and locked the mortise. "It read, 'Dear Sir, please turn a page and let us see the harlot progress a little further.'

"And now, let's progress towards that drink and a snack, Janet. There's a pub at the end of the road which isn't too bad."

"Good." Janet took his arm and they started to walk forward. Behind them the driver of a parked car started his engine.

"How long have you lived with your uncle, Janet?" Tom was only making conversation, but he was careful to omit the "*Miss*". "Many years?"

"Almost twenty, Tom. My parents were both killed in a motor accident when I was 6." The motor of the car ticked over quietly before it was slipped into gear. "After they died, Uncle offered me a home and treated me as his own daughter, though he and my father were never very close.

"A strange man, Tom. I suppose he's brilliant, but certainly not a genius as Mott implied." The car was creeping forward now and following them at a walking pace. "Ruthless, calculating and intensely loyal might be the words to describe him. He'd crush a business rival without mercy, but there's never been a single strike at one of our plants since the firm began." Though they didn't see it, the car began to put on speed. "Three of his original directors were all with him on that tug mentioned in the book. The *Sam and Helen*, which went down in '44." The driver's foot went down on the accelerator and his speed increased. "Since Uncle's first stroke, Peter Kent almost runs the show now, but . . ."

"But look out . . ." The road was crossed by a flyover, there were no lamp-posts to impede the car's progress, but Tom heard it mount the pavement and he swung round and pushed Janet to one side. The headlights were on, pointing them out like targets. Death was rushing towards them and there was nothing to stop it. No doorway to run to, no place to hide.

He covered Janet with his body, but he realized it was a useless gesture, and Mott's voice rang through his head against the roar of the engine. "I think we may expect an attack on your life during the next few hours." He loathed Mott, but the prophecy was coming true. The man or woman who had killed Pike and the publisher's clerk was going to kill again and there was not a single precaution they could take. They clutched each other like lovers and waited for death.

And then suddenly, a miracle happened. The bumpers were within feet of crushing them against the wall when the roar of the engine changed to a scream of brakes and the front wheels swung out and away from them. Tom felt no spine-shattering blow, but only a light tap on the buttocks, as the rear bumper struck him and the car regained the road and accelerated away out of sight. Either a miracle or this eccentric killer had lost his nerve, or changed his mind.

For a long time they leaned against the wall of the flyover, still clinging to each other and thanking whatever fate had saved them. Then they inspected the damage, which was very slight. A small tear across the seat of Tom's trousers, but so what?

Nothing to stop them enjoying the drink they had both wanted, and now really needed.

Eight

Ladyburn was a small, unspoilt village and it didn't take Mott long to locate Honeysuckle Cottage. The house stood at the end of a long, narrow lane and could be described as "olde-Worlde", though in the best sense of the term; Jacobean chimneys, local bricks and tile. He parked the car, climbed out and grinned at a "No Hawkers" sign on the gate and an arrow pointing to the "Tradesman's Entrance". On his present errand, he supposed he might be regarded as a form of trades-man, but the thought that he should use the back door was very amusing indeed. He marched up the garden path and gave the front doorbell a long peal.

"Yes, who are you?" The woman who answered the sum-mons was very tall and very gaunt and wore spectacles and a hearing-aid. She looked about as old as the house itself and eyed Mott with no sign of welcome. "It is very late to be call-ing, so please state your business."

"My name, Miss Marley, is Mott – J. Molden-Mott." He paused to allow this important information to sink in, but the grim expression did not change, so he reluctantly added: "I am here on behalf of Mr Jonathan Pike. You have a book he wishes to buy and I have come to inspect it."

"Stuff and nonsense, man. You are not Mr Pike and there's no resemblance whatsoever."

"I never said I was Pike, madam, but that I am acting on his behalf. My name is J. Molden-Mott and you wrote to Pike only yesterday."

"Nut! a name almost as ridiculous as my own, Mr Nolder-Nut, but I suppose I had better let you in. Wipe your feet on the mat, though. I don't want mud trampled all over the carpet."

Bloody, deaf old crone, Mott thought, but he reluctantly

obeyed and followed Miss Marley into a little, chintzy sitting-room.

"And don't try anything, Mr Nut. I may live alone, but I am very well guarded." The crone nodded and Mott saw a bloated bulldog snoring peacefully before the fire. "One false move and Horatio will sink his teeth through your throat.

"Now, you claim to represent Mr Pike, so identify yourself please."

"Certainly, madam." Though Horatio was fast asleep and had few teeth left to sink, Mott reached in his pocket. "Here is your letter to Pike and here is my own visiting card."

"Thank you, Mr Nut." She glanced at the note, she glanced at his card and then something happened to her. She swayed and staggered towards a *chaise-longue* for support. For a moment he thought Miss Marley was about to have a heart attack and then he looked at her face and recognized the expression. The crone was staring at him with a mixture of awe and adoration and he knew he had found a fan.

"Mott," she said and her voice was barely audible. "You are *the* J. Molden-Mott and I failed to recognize you. Oh, please forgive me, Mr Mott. My eyesight is most unreliable." She fiddled with the hearing-aid's controls, but her eyes were riveted on Mott's face. "But to think that one of the world's greatest authors called on me and I treated him like a criminal – a common felon."

"You have read my works then, Miss Marley?"

"*Have* read them, sir? I read them over and over again and they seem to get fresher and more exciting every time. Look for yourself." With the air of Puss in Boots presenting the Marquis of Carabas with his own riches, she tilted a lamp towards the bookcase and a line of Mott's gaudy volumes glinted back at him. Miss Marley wasn't a crone or a battleaxe, he decided, but a most charming and intelligent woman.

"And, Mr Mott, in spite of my rudeness, I wonder if you would do something terribly kind for me. I know how a man in your position must be pestered by his public, but it would give me so much pleasure if . . ."

"If I would sign a couple for you, dear lady. But of course, Miss Marley." Mott moved towards the case, feeling like the lost heir suddenly revealed – the exiled prince returned to his adoring subjects. In reality his smug smirk bore far more resemblance to that of a tame ape being rewarded with a banana for selecting the longest stick in a pile, but neither he nor his hostess knew that.

"And now, what shall I write?" He pulled out *The Ascent of Mount Mott* and the *Yeti* and considered the problem. "Yes, to Miss Elsie Marley, an ardent admirer. For Elsie Marley, with friendship and affection." He signed both inscriptions with a flourish and handed them to her.

"Mr Mott, this is one of the proudest moments of my life." She looked at the words as though they were from Holy Writ. "No, the very proudest and won't my friends be jealous. You have several admirers in the village and when they see this, they'll . . ."

"Go green with envy, I expect." Mott beamed at her and then glanced at an oil painting above the fireplace. A tall man in naval uniform, gazing into space. "Who is that gentleman, Miss Marley? Looks familiar somehow."

"Oh, only my father, Admiral Archibald Marley. A pleasant man, though cursed with a rather malicious sense of humour, like all my family. He thought it was a joke to christen me Elsie. At school, how I suffered from that vulgar Geordie song and my own name.

"But, here I am chattering about myself and quite forgetting my duties as a hostess. Would you care for a glass of sherry, Mr Mott? There should be a decanter on the sideboard over there."

"Some sherry would be most welcome, Miss Marley." Mott poured out two generous measures. As a rule, he disliked sherry as a drink, but Elsie Marley really was a charming woman. He handed her a glass, pulled up a chair and quite forgot his reason for calling. Miss Marley listened with rapt attention, Horatio, the dog, still snored peacefully and Mott discussed the three topics which really interested him; himself, his exploits and the fate which usually befell his enemies.

"I've known fear, dear lady, what really brave man hasn't, but somehow I've always managed to shrug it aside.

"The others fled and you can't blame 'em, but I stood my ground. The beast weighed over three tons and was travelling at twenty miles an hour but that didn't daunt me. Got him with my trusty forty-five Mannliche, slap through the middle of his tiny brain.

"Blackjack – one of the worst hoodlums in North Africa. Took him by the seat of his pants and tossed him onto the dock. Bust his neck in the fall, and a damn good riddance."

Yes, Mott really enjoyed himself and so did Miss Marley for she thought Mott a fine man; far, far superior in real life to her wildest imaginings. A real British gentleman of a type which had seemed to die out years ago. Miss Marley's early reading had been confined to the hero cult as typified by the writings of Messrs Buchan, Sapper and Rider Haggard and Mott fulfilled all these authors' requirements to the letter. The clock had struck nine when they remembered their business.

"The book you called to collect for Pike, Mr Mott. Yes, I have it all ready for you, though I suppose you're more a customer of Pike's than a friend, and are merely doing him a favour.

"I thought that might be the case, though Pike seemed quite an educated man for a dealer. You'll find the copy on the left of the second shelf, over there."

"Thank you, Miss Marley. Thank you very much indeed." Mott felt a wave of triumph as he inspected the volume, for he'd gone a step forward at last. This was the real McCoy and a mint specimen; not a stain on the vellum cover and no mutilations inside. Every page and illustration was in place and with any luck, they'd tell him what he wanted to know.

But they didn't and his luck had run out, though he couldn't really complain. He had only skipped through the damned book and forgotten most of the contents, but a glance at the index told him he was wrong.

No chapter devoted to the K. 107, and no picture of its designer, Mr J. R. Price, or a hero who had rushed to help the injured. Not a single mention of any mutilated victims or grieving relatives, which was a pity.

Mott had enjoyed the idea of some horribly maimed figure hounding Pike into the grave, of a door opening, and of a hoarse voice croaking, "Don't you recognize me, Mr Price?" Of a charred hand tearing off the mask which concealed some gruesome facial deformities. "What a shame, sir, because you made me what I am and now you're going to feel me." Of the German dagger coming up and Pike going down.

"A ruddy sell-out," Mott thought. "But how curious," he said, struggling to conceal disappointment. "This is quite a rare book, Miss Marley, so how did you manage to acquire two of them."

"Oh, didn't Pike tell you, Mr Mott?" The question seemed to surprise her. "They belonged to my cousin, the Rev'd David Glyde. David worked for the Raeburn Press, as what they call an outside reader, till the firm went out of business.

"Only part-time and as a sort of hobby of course, but I presume he must have been presented with, or got hold of, a couple of copies at some time.

"Poor David! We were never close friends, but it came as a surprise when I heard he had died and left me his library. A nuisance too, as I have very little space, but the vicar, a most helpful man, gave me Pike's address and he came in a taxi and took the lot away. Only paid me fifty pounds, but I was glad to see the back of them."

"But not this copy, dear lady." Mott had finished collating the book and laid it aside. "What happened exactly, Miss Marley?"

"Something you'll scarcely believe, Mr Mott." A trace of Miss Marley's grim expression returned. "Only a week ago, Mrs Shirley Jackson, my daily help; *Shirl* as she wishes to be called, came in and popped the book back on the shelf without a word of apology. "Just borrowed it for a good read, miss, and forgot to return it till now."

"How stupid and careless the lower orders have become, Mr Mott. No respect for their betters or their property whatsoever."

"I entirely agree, my dear lady, but tell me more about your cousin." Mott had no interest in Shirl's reading material, but felt he was on a more interesting scent. "Why should David Glyde want two copies?"

"Only God knows and I take His name seriously, Mr Mott. David was a very perverse character and a clergyman, which made matters worse. There were rumours – horrible rumours, which I don't entirely believe.

"People complained that he'd repeated what he was told in the confessional and joked about them. No, not like my father, Mr Mott." She saw that he was eyeing the admiral's portrait and frowned. "My father had an unfortunate sense of humour, but basically he was on the side of the angels, whereas David . . ." She lowered her voice though there was no eavesdropper to hear the words.

"*Schadenfreude* is the only word to describe David Glyde's lust, Mr Mott. He was possessed by the Devil."

Nine

Schadenfreude – joy derived from another person's despair. Backwards and forwards, deep in thought, Mott paced the floor of his den. A study which might have been decorated by a maniac. Trophies of the chase hung on the walls between archaic, primitive weapons and pictures of the pursuer, and a human skull fitted as a lampshade glowed on the desk.

Schadenfreude. A German word with no real English equivalent, but it told him a lot about the Revd David Glyde. The man really could have been possessed by the Devil, as Miss Marley suggested.

Mott had no faith in the Miltonian conception of Satan. Lucifer, the fallen star of the morning, was a rather noble figure, somewhat like himself, but true evil was small and cruel and vicious. Kipling described the quality well and Mott quoted loudly, though slightly inaccurately, from the Pict's song:

"Mistletoe killing an oak,
Rats gnawing cables in two,
Moths biting holes in a cloak, but
How they must love what they do."

And David Glyde had loved his work all right, especially after the confessional. No direct revelations, of course, and no names mentioned directly. Just hints that certain anonymous individuals suffered from certain objectionable cravings would have been enough to satisfy poor Dave's *Schadenfreude*.

But one stalwart penitent had had such a craving and heard it mentioned by the confessor and sniggered about. The penitent hadn't wasted any time. He'd talked to the rural dean, the rural dean had spoken to the bishop and the sun started to set on the Reverend Mr Glyde.

Not enough evidence to sack or defrock him of course,

and why wash dirty clerical linen in public? "Transfer the fellow. Make him resign his living in Kensington and offer him another where he can do no harm, Canon Fodder."

"Got it, Mr Lord. Just the place, and the patron, Lord Dunsinane, is a very close, personal friend of mine."

So the unjust steward was given a choice and he took it and went north. Very far north to the parish of Glengyle near the tip of Scotland. Glyde couldn't get up to any mischief there, surely. The population were mainly Presbyterians or Roman Catholics and the few C of E members were low church and they didn't believe in confession. The Revd Glyde should have rotted quietly among the rocks and the heather, following his part-time occupation as a publisher's reader and so he did till he died. But he left his cousin a legacy.

And there was nothing to be learned from the damned book – nothing at all. Mott had searched the pages a dozen times and found not a single incriminating thing, though some of the illustrations were slightly interesting. "The last moments of the frigate *River Madoc* and the rescue tug *Sam*. This picture was taken from the *Sam's* lifeboat just before the start of her epic voyage home."

"The bodies of the three climbers who fell from the East face of Ben S'Gurr in 1947. The only survivor of this accident was Sir Roland Rawson who despite severe personal injuries crawled fifteen miles to summon help."

Mott hated Roland Rawson and that photograph had interested him at first, but there was nothing in it to tarnish Rawson's unfortunately untarnished reputation. There was nothing sinister in Levin's death book, though he wasn't sure what he was looking for. Some suggestion of a crime committed years ago perhaps – some hint of a family skeleton which could drive an unbalanced mind to mass murder. He turned to the chapter on his enemy Rawson again and frowned at the text.

The East face of Ben S'Gurr is a seven hundred foot wall

starting from Lob's Chimney. I was the last member of the team and securely attached to a flake of rock inside the chimney. I could not see the rest of the party above because of an overhanging chockstone. The rock of the wall itself is loose and treacherous however and I can only assume that Hal James, the leader, fell near the crest and pulled Wakefield and West from their belays.

The rope parted with the force of their triple descent and broke my collar bone and fractured three ribs, but . . .

But with superhuman courage and fortitude Roland Rawson had ignored his own injuries and climbed down the chimney alone. He had examined the dead bodies of his companions and set off, staggered off and crawled off to summon help.

Possible, Mott supposed. Though he disliked Rawson intensely, he couldn't deny that the fellow was a tough cookie, but . . .

But had the leaders fallen or were they pulled? Rawson could have untied the rope, administered a sharp tug and down would have come cradle and baby and all.

Yes, that was possible. Anything was possible where characters like Rawson were concerned. But why, what rational motive could he have for killing three apparently inoffensive human beings? Gain, no. Roland Rawson was an independently wealthy man. Blackmail possibly, if one of the party had discovered something discreditable about him. Mere pique – sheer ill-temper; that was the most probable cause. Mott fancied he could read Rawson's character like a book and the man was a dirty book and subject to ungovernable rages. Any unfortunate joke at his expense might have triggered off anger and sent the party hurtling down to the scree. Rawson could have slipped in the chimney himself and cracked those ribs and his collar-bone during the fall, but where did the book fit in?

Dawn was up, the sun was shining and Mott switched off the skull lamp and carried the volume over to a window. The picture of the three corpses was too small to show much detail, but if the photograph was blown up and magnified, if the enlarged print proved that the rope had not snapped but been untied, he'd hold Sir Roland Rawson in the palm of his hand.

A pleasant thought and he considered the blighter's career, for he and Rhino Rawson had been rivals since boyhood. At school each striving for the title victor ludorum and cheating on the way. At university each struggling to place chamber-pots on a higher steeple than the other before being sent down by a long-suffering but exasperated authority.

The final break had come ten years ago when both claimed to have discovered the source of a certain African river. As it happened, both claims were proved wrong by a French helicopter pilot, but Rawson got the credit and a knighthood, before the truth was revealed. Mott had never forgiven him for that and he wasn't allowed to forget the title, either. Every Christmas a vulgar card arrived bearing greetings to *Mister* Molden-Mott from *Sir* Roland-Rawson KCMG.

Yes, it would be very pleasant to reveal Rhino as an insane murderer and have him locked away in The Village of Irons. Mott grinned at the thought and then frowned as the telephone rang.

"J. Molden-Mott speaking." He lifted the receiver and recognized Tom's voice. "Yes, Mayne, I have the book, but it's no use to us at the moment and this is what I want you to do." His smile returned because an idea had occurred to him. "Is there a reputable public auction in London next week?

"Thursday at the Foden Gallery. Yes, that should give us time and here are my instructions. Put *Men of Courage* up for sale at Foden's and see that it's well advertised. Also make sure that there's a thumping reserve on the price. A couple of thousand should be adequate." A contemptible trick really, like shooting a sitting bird, he thought, but if Rawson swallowed it, they'd have him on toast. Mott would have much preferred a more dramatic denouement, but one needed a long spoon to sup with a devil.

"Yes, my copy of *Courage* is in mint condition, Mayne, and you can rely on that.

"What are you trying to tell me?" He listened to Tom's account of his early adventure. The car charging under the flyover, mounting the pavement and turning aside at the last possible moment. "No, old boy, I don't think some drunk lost control of his vehicle for a moment. The driver was your executioner all right and he didn't change his mind or have a twinge of conscience. A rum thing that he didn't kill you then and there, so take care of yourself till next Thursday. My bank will look after the book, in the meanwhile.

"Yes, until Thursday morning. This is one of the very few copies still in existence and our pal will not get his grubby hands on it before I give the word." He banged down the phone and returned to the window. A pleasant day and the long-range forecast was favourable for at least a week. Ample time to bring his murderer to bay without the sales-room deception.

An objectionable murderer and an objectionable blackmailer. Old David Glyde had run through the proofs and the illustrations and seen that the rope had not been cut, but untied. As his cousin said Mr Glyde was possessed by the Devil, and the Devil was a strong tempter.

Though not as powerful as J. Molden-Mott, God was always on the side of the just and God and Mott were acting together. They would see that justice was done, but first things came first. Photostat the book and magnify the illustrations, lodge the copy in his bank and then off to the wilds of Scotland.

Ten

"No – no – no, Mr Mayne. Not on your nelly!" Gordon Glover, manager and chief auctioneer of the Foden Gallery and Sales Rooms, frowned at Tom's request and lowered his rump against what had been described to him as a genuine Sheraton writing-desk: a desk which creaked in protest and he wouldn't have cared if it had fallen apart. One glance inside the drawers had proved that whatever the owner might say, the thing was a fake and a pretty poor fake too. He would see that it was returned COD that very afternoon. The Foden was not a place to suffer junk gladly.

"Quite out of the question, I'm afraid – most irregular." Glover wore a black suit, relieved by a dove-grey tie, and had an air of immense dignity: the kind of man one associated with Masonic functions, and after-lunch speeches of interminable length; of hearty platitudes directed against the younger generation; the kind of man one would like to see sit down on a tack.

"You should know us well enough by now, Mr Mayne. You can be sure that we would help if it were possible. Hold back a cheque for a few days, arrange for a private view and the Foden would always, always be sympathetic towards a good and valued customer.

"But this scheme is preposterous and smacks of fraud or criminal intent. I'm surprised that you should have made such a request. To ask a firm with a reputation built up over three generations of fair dealing and respect to offer a book which we have never even seen or collated is tantamount to . . ." Like a river in flood, the platitudes rolled grandly out till Tom intervened.

"Mr Glover, you have my word that the book is in mint condition and will be delivered on time." He fought back irritation because he realized Glover's predicament. Mott had decided that *Men of Courage* should be kept in a bank till the morning of the sale and it was asking a lot for Glover to advertize it unseen. All the same, Glover was a pompous, self-important ass and it would do no harm to deflate his dignity. Tucked away in Tom's mind was a piece of information which could ruin Mr Glover and tarnish the Foden's reputation. He had no wish to use the knowledge, but the weapon was there.

"Your word, Mr Mayne, is a very good word, but you must consider our point of view." If an elephant could speak Tom imagined it would sound equally pompous and pedantic. "My brother-in-law, a rather common sort of man I'm sorry to say, manages a public house near Epsom and has similar problems to face. He would benefit by cashing cheques for his better class of customers, but if he did so, all the local riff-raff would try to follow suit. You are attempting to put the gallery in a similar predicament Mr Mayne, and I'm afraid that I must refuse." Glover had no trunk to swing, but Tom pictured him swinging one. "You will appreciate that the request is hardly ethical and you cannot expect the Foden to get involved in anything of a dishonest nature."

"No, I suppose not." A car backfired in the street and Tom started slightly. Mott's warnings that the killer would strike again seemed very real. Everyone who spoke to him, every sudden movement or noise, seemed like a threat and his nerves were like raw wounds. He had done what Mott asked him to do, not even discussing the plan with Janet, and the trap was almost sprung. Only this pompous elephant – No, not an elephant, they are supposed to have a sense of humour. This bone-headed water-buffalo of a man stood in his way.

"Of course not, my dear chap. Why, in almost a hundred years of business, Foden's have never been mixed up in anything underhand or shady." A loud creak came from the desk and Glover raised his buttocks up from it. He didn't mind breaking the so-called Sheraton, but a fall would be a blow to his dignity, and it was time to show this persistent young man that the interview was over. He pulled a gleaming half-hunter watch from his pocket and glanced meaningfully at the dial.

"Just think what you have asked me to do, Mr Mayne. To advertize a book in our next catalogue without even examining its condition or putting the thing on view. No, no that's quite impossible."

"But I have promised you that the book is in excellent order and will get to you in good time." Tom was reaching the end of his tether, because the man really was a buffalo. A great, self-righteous, pompous buffalo, browsing suspiciously beside some muddy stream.

" 'Pollicitis dives quilibet esse potest.' As Ovid said, anyone can be rich in promises, and the reserve you wish to place on the item; two thousand pounds." Glover raised a flabby, white hand to emphasize the sum. "An absurd amount and I know that there's something fishy about the prices those *Men of Courage* have reached in the last few months. Something very suspicious, which the Foden Gallery cannot be party to." He moved slowly towards the door and Tom suddenly imagined himself in a Mottish role. Buffaloes are probably the most dangerous beasts in the jungle. Even a lion steers clear of them, but one accurate shot through the brain . . .

"But don't think I'm accusing you of dishonesty, Mr Mayne. You are merely the agent of some eccentric client who is trying to prey upon your youth and inexperience." Glover paused with his hand on the doorknob. "If you are still gullible enough to continue with this scheme, approach another firm of auctioneers. Somerlees of Reaker and Smith might agree, though personally I doubt it."

"But Bronte or the Countess of Hertford would, Mr Glover." The buffalo was in range now and Tom prepared to squeeze the trigger. "Yes, I came to you because we're friends, Mr Glover, and I wonder what that prayer-book was finally sold for. A thousand, or more?"

"Nothing like that, and the countess was perfectly satisfied with the total proceeds." The hunted had scented the hunter and was uncertain whether to charge or beat a hasty retreat. "And you were satisfied, Mr Mayne. You said so at the time and I gave you two hundred quid for the tip-off. You wouldn't, you couldn't, be base enough to betray me."

"I might be, Mr Glover." Tom saw that the buffalo had decided that discretion was the better part of valour and Glover pulled out a notebook and a fountain-pen. "One copy of *Men of Courage* numbered 'twelve', Raeburn Press, limited edition 1958. Make it the last lot of the day and don't forget the reserve." Tom watched Glover write down his instructions and thought of another transaction completed three years ago.

One couldn't blame the Countess of Hertford or her librarian for not noticing that the prayer-book was inscribed. They wanted to make room on their shelves for other volumes and five hundred goats found their way to the Foden.

Not a bad set of goats and one member of the flock had a message on the flyleaf. Tiny handwriting as though somebody was trying to copy out the Lord's Prayer on a postage stamp. Even Tom was confused at first, but he consulted Glover and Glover consulted a member of the Bronte Society. The prayer-book was withdrawn from the auction and sold privately and without the countess's knowledge. She got a pound, Tom got two hundred pounds and God only knew what Glover received.

A little leather-bound book of devotion with two lines of faded, cramped writing to give it value; "To Charlotte, from her loving Sister Emily."

Eleven

"Evil, Mr Molden-Mott? Nay, it's not for me to explain how the Prince of Darkness spins his web, but I will say this." James Gourlay, proprietor of the Moorcock Inn at Glengyle paused impressively. "The Reverend Glyde was a very fearsome man."

"Fearsome is not an exact description of character, so please amplify your statement." Mott leaned against the bar and downed his third double whisky. "How did David Glyde inspire fear, Mr Gourlay? Any definite instances?"

"Well, let me think for a moment, sir." Gourlay eyed his guest with mixed feelings. He hadn't liked the look of Mott when he arrived, well after closing time last night, and demanded a room. He'd resented being threatened with legal action if a room was not provided. He had disliked being treated as Mott's hired servant and told that the bed was damp, the accommodation too small and the breakfast inedible.

Only during the last half hour had his opinion started to alter, for there was no denying that Mott was a good listener. Everything that happened at Glengyle seemed to interest him and Jimmy Gourlay liked to talk. "Badness is a difficult thing to identify, sir. I mean, if you rob me till for gain, you deserve to be punished, but if you steal for the fun of depriving me, that's a different matter.

"Call a man *raca* and you're in danger of the judgement. Call him a fool and you face hell-fire. And David Glyde is in hell now, if Christ is any judge."

"Instances, Gourlay. Concrete examples of Glyde's perversity, and get me a refill while you think about them." Mott drained his glass and pushed it across the counter. "Any cruelty to animals, children or old people for instance?"

"Not to animals or bairns, sir, but there was that shockin'

affair regarding Mary Mollinson, and the way he treated Sir Roland.

"Abominable, what he did to Mary. She'd been the old vicar's housekeeper for nigh on thirty years and the manse was the only home she knew. But Glyde said she wasn't up to her work and she'd have to go.

"She did in a sense. Telephoned Dr Angus to come over and he found her in the kitchen with a knife through her breast. You may not believe this, sir, but when the doctor told Glyde she was dead, he just grinned.

"Sir Roland, Mr Mott? That could have been almost as bad, but Roland Rawson was a harder nut to crack." Gourlay had refilled the glass and placed it on the counter. "He threatened to take a horsewhip to Glyde if he repeated those hellish rumours and might have done given the chance. But Glyde was lying at the bottom of Ben S'Gurr with his head stove in when Sir Roland got back to Scotland."

"Murder?" Mott leaned forward. Everything that discredited Roland Rawson interested him and he knew what the rumours were. Three men had died on that mountain and a fiend was responsible. "Was Rawson suspected of killing Glyde?"

"Oh no, and what an idea!" Gourlay shook his head. "Sir Roland has a wee croft up the glen which he uses for holidays and suchlike, but he wasn't here when Glyde was found. Up in the Arctic Circle Sir Roland was, looking for a rare species of the great white whale."

"Which I did discover, Gourlay, and the skull is now lodged in the Natural History Museum, London." Gourlay had been overheard and the discoverer strutted into the bar. "And you – you're here, Mr Mott. What a coincidence! We haven't met for years. Not since the day I saved your life from that lion in Africa." Sir Roland Rawson was shorter and less bulky than Mott, but he looked equally formidable and was dressed in an anorak, bright yellow trousers and a pair of climbing boots. "Yes, I will have a drink as you're kind enough to ask." He accepted an offer which had not been made and clambered up onto a bar stool. "A pint of bitter please, Gourlay, if your beer's not off again."

"My beer's never off, Sir Roland," Gourlay muttered, but Rawson didn't hear him. He beamed at Mott and then prodded him in the ribs with a finger. "Good grief. You're putting a bit of weight on, old chap. Getting very flabby. Have to do something about that, and you've come to the right place. I'm on my way to have a bit of a scramble on Ben S'Gurr and would be delighted if you'd join me."

"Go scrambling with you?" Mott's hand trembled as he lifted his whisky glass. He'd come to Scotland to expose a murderer and the murderer was there at the bar beside him. A cold-blooded killer had invited him to climb the very mountain on which he had once taken three human lives and now hoped to take his own. "No, I'm sorry, Rawson," he said. "But I'm rather busy today."

"You're not busy, but scared, old boy." Sir Roland had distinctly read his thoughts. "Gourlay's been talking and you've been listening, eh? You believe those rumours spread about by our vile, unlamented parson. You think I pulled those blighters off the East Face, and could do the same to you." He started to lift his pint pot and then laid it down on the counter. "No, Sir Roland Rawson does not drink with cowards or fools and you appear to be both those things, Mr Molden-Mott."

"Nobody can call me a coward and get away with it, Rawson." Mott flushed with rage and knocked back his Scotch. "Finish your beer and I'll be changed and ready to join you in ten minutes flat."

Though he was too angry to know it, Mott might soon be changing his clothes for a shroud.

"Implications – insinuations – unfounded poppycock." They had left Rawson's Land-Rover at the end of the glen and while toiling up the scree Sir Roland talked. "I saw through our spiritual advisor the moment I clapped eyes on him, Mott, and the Revd Mr Glyde was a wrong 'un.

"Tried to filch my good name, but I had the evidence to prove him a liar. After those three chaps went for a Burton, I kept the rope and it's still hanging up in my cottage. The ends show that the strands snapped twenty feet from my shoulder, and you can have a squint for yourself.

"If I don't decide to tug you off first of course, and add to my list of misdeeds." They had reached the crags and Rawson paused and chuckled. "To think that you, an old friend and admirer, could imagine that I was a callous murderer.

"Well, your act fooled me, old boy. The joke was at my expense and let's get going." He removed a nylon line from his shoulder and started to unfold the coils. "Bit of a breeze blowing up, so watch out for those belays on the face. All pretty rotten and crumbling as my pals learned to their cost.

"Alternative pitches, or do you want me to lead all the way?"

"Alternative, Rawson." Mott tied on the rope and tried to control his expression. He no longer believed that Rawson was a murderer, but to be considered an admirer rankled considerably. "Get rid of this Scotch first, though. Won't be a second." He urinated noisily against the rocks, but Rawson was already on his way. Feet planted firmly on every hold, hands reaching for supports and body correctly balanced. The man might be an insolent beast, but there was no denying that he was an excellent climber.

But so had Glyde been, apparently. Mott thought about what Rawson had told him in the car. The old boy was well over 60 but he had scrambled over the hills like a ruddy cat on the tiles.

Why? Why does a man climb a mountain? "Because it's there," said George Mallory. Mott echoed the thoughts of Inspector Pounder to Tom. "Because I have had a dream," said Sherpa Tensing Norgay. "For Germany," replied Toni and Adolf Schmidt, the Bavarian cyclists and perhaps the greatest of them all. "For the glory and honour of J. Molden-Mott and to run down a mass murderer," thought Mott, as the rope tugged. Rawson had completed the first pitch and was waiting for him to follow.

"Good exercise, old boy? No real difficulties yet." Rawson was seated on a ledge with the rope securely belayed to a pillar. "The next stage veers to the right and ends up under the chimney. Only fifty-five feet, but have a bit of a breather first. You look shagged out, and I don't want another death on my conscience."

"I am perfectly fit, thank you, and will proceed." Mott moved out onto a flake. The route was clearly marked by the old scratches of climbing boots and the breeze was his only problem. A gusty wind had blown in from the Atlantic which tugged his anorak, but caused no real trouble. In under five minutes he was tied up to a belay below the chimney and bellowing for Rawson to join him.

"Lovely view, ain't it?" To Mott's disgust, Rawson appeared with a cigarette dangling between his lips. "Nothing but the Isle of Lewis between us and the Nantucket Light. The chimney's rather a sweat but nothing to worry about. The worries start later." He spat out the cigarette and started the sweat. An almost classical chimney over eighty feet long, but just the right diameter. With his back against one wall and his feet on the other, Roland Rawson was in no danger unless he suffered a heart attack, and Mott paid out the rope and consulted a climbing guide.

The East Face of Ben S'Gurr presents few difficulties apart from the last two pitches which gives the climb a rating of *Very Severe*. This was established during a tragic triple accident in 1952.

After leaving the Great Chimney, the route turns to the right and proceeds up an exposed and almost vertical wall of a hundred and fifty feet in length. At eighty foot, the leader may decide to belay, but as there is no adequate stance and the rocks are loose and crumbling, it is better to complete the climb and treat the pitches as one. Sea bird droppings are at times a nuisance, and the leader cannot be adequately protected by his Number Two below.

"Come on, old boy. I'm ready." The leader bellowed and Number Two tucked away the book and began to mount the chimney. He took his time about it, and not because of physical exertion or natural hazards. Vertical and exposed walls, loose rocks and sea-bird droppings meant nothing to a man like him, but there was the human element to consider. Rawson – Sir Roland Rawson, a suspected murderer. Just a tug, a twitch on the rope and J. Molden-Mott would go crashing down to death and the scree.

"Ah, there you are at last, Mott." The suspected murderer beamed at him. Rawson was securely attached to the chockstone which straddled the chimney, and he didn't look like a killer. He looked like a hearty, middle-aged man who was thoroughly enjoying himself.

"A sweat, as I said, but now the troubles start and the wind's increasing." He looked through the gap below the wedged stone and shrugged his shoulders. "Can't promise to hold you if you fall, so shall I take on from here again? You're clearly worn out and look slightly seedy, but I'm in the pink of condition and know this cliff like the back of me hand."

"Clearly worn out" – "slightly seedy" – "pink of condition" – "back of me hand". The words might or might not have been insolent, but Mott felt insulted and he checked that the bowline around his waist was tightly knotted.

"I am perfectly capable of completing this pitch, Rawson," he said, "and I intend to do so now."

"Then watch your step, old boy," Rawson advised, but the advice was not taken. Mott had already stepped through the gap and was on the wall.

Rawson had noticed that the wind was increasing and he was right. The author of the guide-book had explained the difficulties and Mott couldn't deny them. The cliff was hellishly exposed and seemed to be craned out over the sea. The rock was loose and rotten and the angle was damn near vertical. Every foothold seemed to be coated with sea-bird droppings and the birds themselves whirled, screeching around him like harpies. Probably they imagined he was after their nests, but that did nothing to cheer Mott on. The rope connecting him to Rawson sagged and tugged in the gale. Once a lump of stone gave way between his fingers and vanished into space. Once his boots almost slipped from a ledge, but at last he found a resting-place.

The guide-book reported that the first belay had not enough stance to rely on and should be ignored. But there was an overhanging rock above his head to provide a hold and he slipped a line round it and clipped it to his rope with a carabina. Just a few seconds' rest, he thought. Just a couple of minutes to get my breath back. He closed his eyes for a moment and then turned and looked out to sea. Nothing of interest except a boat, dipping and rolling on the swell five hundred yards away from the shore.

No, he was wrong. His eyes had been fixed on the rock and they weren't focusing correctly. The object wasn't rising or falling on the sea, it was stationary and riveted to the sea bed. It might look like the bows of a sinking vessel, but that was another illusion. The thing was an island, a stone pillar only just visible above the tide and he'd seen that pillar somewhere, though he didn't know where.

Mott had never been near Glengyle before and he'd never climbed Ben S'Gurr, but he recognized that tiny island though for no reason he could imagine. A painting – a postcard or a photograph. There were several possibilities, but he had to be sure and there was a camera dangling around his neck. He could and would take a photograph; just for interest, just to refresh his memory, just . . . Just for curiosity.

A little more to the right was needed to get the island into perspective and he leaned right and never heard his belay creak in protest. Only a scrap more, the carabina would hold him. That's it, his finger pressed the trigger, the rope below jerked, and the rock above his head slid forward.

Mott never realized what was happening till it was too late. A sledge-hammer seemed to split his skull – the sun vanished.

"Extraordinary! The fellow must have a cranium like a ruddy ape and it's a miracle he survived." The words seemed to come from a long way away off and Mott opened his eyes expecting to see the face of God smiling down at him. He didn't. All he saw was a fierce old man with white hair and weather-beaten cheeks scowling over the pillow.

"And he's coming round, Rhino – quite remarkable." The aged face registered complete astonishment. "Must have hit that ridge at over forty miles an hour before your rope caught him. Constitution of an ox and beyond all my medical experience.

"What's that? No, don't try to talk, Mr Mott. Not yet." Dr Duncan Angus, the local GP, looked at the figure on the bed with professional curiosity. "Let's just check your reactions first. Does this hurt at all?" He gave the patient a sharp blow in the ribs and was rewarded with an instant reaction. Mott gave a howl of anguish and tried to pull himself up the bed. "It does, eh! Excellent, miraculous in fact. No damage to the nervous system and no bones broken either. Give your pal a drop of brandy, Rhino, though add plenty of water."

"Brandy – from a bloody assassin!" Mott saw Rawson cross the room and reach for a bottle. "I don't know who you are, sir, but that man tried to kill me. Jerked me off the rocks while I was talking a photograph and . . ."

"And then caught you on the rope after a fall of over a hundred feet." Dr Angus registered astonishment. "No, sir, Sir Roland saved your life. Rhino lowered you to the ground and carried you to his Land-Rover, Mr Mott. He telephoned me for help and as a local medical man I naturally came at once. You slipped off the cliff or the belay came away when you were taking that picture. Sir Roland deserves thanks, not mindless recriminations."

"Humph!" Mott had no intention of thanking Rhino, but he risked a sip of brandy. "I was photographing an island," he said, and wondered whether his camera was still intact. "A little point of rock about a mile from the shore. I know I'd seen that point somewhere in the past, though I can't say where. Any idea what the thing is, Doctor? Any local stories connected with it?"

"The Hag of Foulda?" Angus held out the glass again. "Plenty of legends about the old hag, but most of 'em go too far back to be credited. A notorious risk for shipping, as she's under water at high tide, but why are you interested in the hag, Mr Mott?

"Oh, I know you were talking to Gourlay about David Glyde before Rhino met you. I was having a dram in the pub when he rang up for assistance, and James Gourlay is a great gossip. He told me about your interest in Glyde, and I'd like to hear more, Mr Mott."

"Not sure what to say, Doctor." The brandy was making Mott feel better and he was glad to hear Rhino groan and see him rub his shoulder. With any luck the rope might have damaged his collar-bone again when he caught him. Good show – the man might not be a murderer, but he was a damned objectionable fellow. "No, can't be sure, but a cousin of Glyde's, Miss Elsie Marley, a most intelligent woman, told me that your vicar was shifted up here after some trouble in London and she asked me to make a few enquiries regarding his death." Though Mott's head still throbbed the lie came fluently and easily. "You were one of his close friends, Doctor, so tell me what happened – fill me in."

"Well, I wouldn't describe meself as a friend, Mr Mott." Angus's white hair fluttered as he shook his head. "Davie Glyde wasn't a man to make friends easily; far too bitter and sour for that. Felt that life had let him down and he'd failed both as a priest and a publisher's reader.

"Quite an amusing old cove in a way when he wasn't feeling sorry for himself, though that was not often. Said or implied that there was something in a book he'd edited that could make a lot of people sweat blood. Never told me what it was, but I suspected – only suspected – that it was somehow connected with the Hag of Foulda."

"And you could be right, Doc." In spite of his discomfort Rawson decided to put an oar in. "Glyde was always pottering about on Ben S'Gurr, chuckling at times when he looked at that rock; chuckling and rubbing his hands together.

"Once I stopped him and asked the cause of his amusement and he replied with a twisted text cribbed from the scriptures. 'Sir Roland Rawson, they hate me with cause.'

"Never knew what he meant – never discovered who they were, but somebody got Glyde in the end. In spite of what your son and the police thought, we know better eh, Doc."

"The official version was that Davie Glyde had slipped, knocked his head on a lump of rock and been drowned when the tide came in, though I knew it was murder.

"How did I know, Mr Mott?" Angus scowled at the interruption. "I may be an elderly man, but I've still got a pair of eyes in my head and the intelligence to use 'em, whatever my fool of a son and the police surgeon from Inverness may have said to the contrary. They believed that natural decomposition and the action of sea creatures accounted for David's injuries, but I knew better. Got a pair of pliers handy, Rhino?"

"Of course." Rawson hurried to a cupboard and produced them.

"Good! Now hold out your right hand, Mr Mott, and I'll show you." He gripped one of Mott's fingers between the jaws and gave a slight squeeze. "Yes, that hurts, doesn't it, but not a tenth as much as Glyde suffered. David was tortured before he died, you see." He released the grips and smiled. "Some bastards crushed his fingers with screws – thumbscrews."

Twelve

"No, Janet. Nothing from Mott as yet, but we can only hope. And talking about that, what news about your uncle. Any improvement?"

"Not really, and if I didn't know him, I'd think he wants to die or has lost the will to live." Janet considered the complexities of human nature. "Also the wish for salvation, you might say, and he's already made his funeral arrangements quite clear, as Peter Kent explained to me this morning. Uncle does not wish for burial or cremation. He wants his body to be weighted down with chains and dumped into the sea from *Bully Boy*.

"I'm not sure that the arrangement is even legal, but that's what Uncle wants and I won't try to stop him. No priest, no funeral service, no last rites; a sort of Viking end, with his original crew around him, though they and the *Bully* won't join in the final plunge.

"The *Bully Boy*! Oh, she's an old motor yacht which he bought soon after the war as a sort of memorial to the tugboat *Sam*. He and his fellow survivors from the *Sam* took the *Bully* everywhere when they had the chance, which wasn't often and there are only three left now.

"Peter and Uncle and . . ." She broke off as the shop door opened. "But I'm interrupting you and you've got a customer."

"So I have, Janet, and a rather embarrassing one." Tom stood up and smiled at the woman in the doorway, who was old and thin and clutched a brief-case. "Ah, Mrs Rayner. Got a few more books you wish to sell?"

"Yes, Mr Mayne, and you'll be pleased to have these: the pick of Jeffrey's collection." She lifted the case onto a shelf and opened it to reveal a treasure trove. An imagined trove and Tom's heart sank as he looked at the titles. *Sixty Years a Queen –*

With the Flag to Pretoria – The Collected Works of Sir Walter Scott with at least three volumes missing. Also two rather pretty copies of *Roger's Selected Poetry*, but who read Roger's today?

"I'm sorry, Mrs Rayner," he said. "But I'm afraid I can't use these. They're not bad books, of course, but I've got too much similar stock on my shelves as you can see. One copy of *Sixty Years*, two of *With the Flag* and . . ."

"They are very good books, Mr Mayne. Jeffrey, my husband, bought them himself and he was a great collector and knew what he was doing." The woman was not only small and old, but she looked tired and frightened and Tom remembered her husband well. A man who liked certain subjects and thought everyone else did. A retired clerk who came into the shop at least once a week and left clutching a volume Tom was glad to see the back of.

Well, Jeffrey Rayner was dead now and he'd left his widow nothing except memories, a small pension and a collection of junk he'd imagined to be bargains. And debts, of course. The rates were overdue, the gas and the electricity bills had to be settled, so Mrs Rayner had pulled a little pile from the shelves, thinking she had at least some capital.

"And most of them came from your shop, Mr Mayne," she said, opening the cover of *Sixty Years a Queen*. "That's your mark, isn't it?"

"Yes, that was my price, Mrs Rayner." Tom winced at the amount he had charged and then tried to explain the working of his trade. How one only bought run-of-the-mill items in the hope that there might be a few readily saleable volumes amongst them. That the rest would sit on the shelves in the hope of finding a mug who might buy them and the rest would then be thrown into sacks and sent away to be pulped.

He couldn't use the word '*mug*' of course, and he didn't get the chance – Janet intervened. "May I have a look?" she said and flicked through the collection. "No, not bad, madam, and would you accept thirty pounds for the lot?"

"Thank you, miss. Thirty will be just right." Mrs Rayner

almost snatched the notes out of Janet's hand. "And as you seem to be Mr Mayne's partner, you might come round and see what else I've got at home. My Jeffrey knew what he was up to and there's some really valuable stuff; genuine *first editions*, some of 'em." Like many uninformed persons, she used the term 'first edition' as though it was some kind of lucky charm or prayer.

"I'd love to come and look at them, Mrs Rayner," Janet answered and smiled. "Have you got the lady's telephone number, Tom?"

"Good, then I'll give you a ring in a day or two, madam." She held open the door as the woman closed her case and departed in triumph.

"Why?" Tom could only gape at her. "Thirty quid for a pile of rubbish which isn't worth as many pence. You must be mad, Janet, even if you are rich. Partners indeed! It will be a long time before I sign any agreement with you, my dear. You'd have me out of business before I was . . ." He glanced at one title and scowled. "Before I was sixty seconds a bookseller."

"Sorry, Tom. I know that woman will brag about the price I paid her, and you'll get more rubbish offered because of what she got, but don't – please don't begrudge me a little moment of charity." She returned to the desk and sat down. "The woman looked so pathetic and lost and I couldn't really help myself."

"Well, don't worry. No real harm done as long as you don't want me to repay you out of the till." Tom moved to join her and then turned as the door opened again and a man he didn't recognize for a moment appeared. "Can I help you, sir," he said and then saw who the visitor was. "You – where the hell have you been?"

"Yes, me, Mayne." Mott stepped forward and he looked quite different. He walked with a limp and had a stick to help him. His left eye was black and a bandage encircled his forehead.

"Home is the sailor – home from the sea, and the hunter

home from the hill." He spoke cynically, but his manner had changed too. All his normal arrogance had vanished and he sounded abject and almost apologetic. "Hill is the reason for my delay, as it happens. Fell off a blasted mountain in Scotland. Damn near broke my neck and for no good reason as far as I'm aware. Followed a wild-goose chase and discovered that the goose was a ruddy duck.

"But, you're here, Miss Vale. My apologies for not seeing you at once, but with one eye temporarily out of action, you must forgive the lapse."

He eased himself into Tom's chair and groaned. "So very sorry to hear on the plane radio that your uncle has shown no sign of improvement to date, but not to worry unduly. The sun always rises given time, and we've got the time.

"Got till tomorrow, Mayne, because your auctioneer pal has played ball. He slowly reached in his pocket and drew out a copy of Foden's catalogue. *Men of Courage*, adequately described and the last lot in the sale. No mention of the reserve price of course, and that's going to bring our killer into the sights.

"Oh yes, there's a killer all right, Miss Vale. Don't know his name or his motive, but I do know he exists." He paused as the phone rang and Tom picked up the receiver. "Mayne speaking. Yes, she's here and please hang on a moment. Someone called Kent, for you, Janet."

"Thank you, Tom. I left your number just in case my uncle had a turn for the worse." She took the instrument from him and spoke very slowly. "Janet Vale speaking, Peter. Yes – yes. I see, and I should be there in half an hour. Goodbye for the present." She replaced the instrument, and there was a hint of tears in her eyes.

"Must go, Tom. He's still alive but moving to the *Bully Boy* up the Thames." She picked up her handbag, and eased back the chair. "The Viking's funeral will shortly begin."

"Just a precaution, Miss Janet." Peter Kent stood in the *Bully*

Boy's saloon, and he tried to appear cheerful but failed. "The chief may live for months – years even – according to the specialists, but he wanted to be sure of dying afloat.

"And what better place is there to die? The chief, your uncle, bought the *Bully* out of his gratuity in 1946 and she was his base and our home for wellnigh three years till the business started to grow.

"Lord, what years they were, miss. Planning, scheming and gathering in every penny piece we could lay our hands on, but they paid off. The chief and survivors of the old *Sam* saw that they paid."

The chief! Janet almost shuddered, because the term had no connection with what she had seen in the cabin. Sir Simon Vale had not even recognized her. He lay on his bunk with Mackenzie in attendance and he was deaf, sightless and speechless. A human cabbage, ready and ripe for death.

"Yes, they paid, Miss Janet." Kent's voice interrupted her thoughts. "Seven plants in operation once the Wandsworth buildings are completed, next June. Five thousand hands on the payroll and the last dividend stood at a hundred and nine, yesterday. Not a bad achievement for a few merchant seamen to have made."

"Merchant seamen, Peter?" Janet frowned at him. "But I always imagined my uncle was in the navy."

"So he was, Miss. Gunnery lieutenant, but apart from the gunners all those big ocean-going tugs had mercantile marine crews including the sick-bay attendants. The master was killed when the *Sam* went down, so the chief took over on the lifeboat."

"I'm sorry what happened just now, miss." As though in answer to Kent's voice, Mackenzie appeared in the alleyway. "The chief was having one of his bad turns when you arrived, but they come and go and he'll recognize you now. Asked to see you, in fact, Miss Janet, so please have a word with him."

"Of course, Bill." Janet hurried past him towards the cabin and hardly believed what she saw at first. Her uncle was up and standing by the open porthole. He wore pyjamas and a dressing-gown, his shoulders were as straight as ever and his hair was neatly combed. "Ah, there you are at last, girl. Taken your time getting here, but shut the door and sit down." He turned and looked at her and his eyes were very bright and he had recently been shaved.

"That's better, and we're going to have a little chat, my dear. Won't take long. I'll probably pass out again in a few minutes, so listen carefully." His voice was harsh and rasping – a voice she had never heard before. "First, I've got a question to ask. Do you believe that the Devil may take human form?"

"No, Uncle, I don't." Janet frowned and considered the problem. "I think there is an impersonal force of evil which can infect certain individuals or groups, but . . ."

"Yes, that's the kind of meaningless reply I might have expected, Janet." He interrupted her before she could finish the sentence. "Both your parents would have spoken in the same way. Two liberal-minded schoolteachers who always infuriated me. Glad that car happened to crash and killed 'em.

"Happened to crash, Uncle?" He had accentuated the word and Janet leaned forward.

"Happened, or was made to, Janet. What does it matter?" He dismissed the point with a flick of his thumb. "Your father (my brother) was a socialist who didn't believe in private enterprise. Wouldn't have anything to do with our business. Couldn't bring himself to congratulate me when I got a knighthood. Glad he died with your mother, because that's how I got you, Janet.

"Brother Ted claimed that power corrupts, and so it can, though not as much as poverty and illness. But you'll never be poor, Janet. I've seen to that.

"Transferred ninety per cent of my shares into your name, five years ago; just in time to avoid death duties.

"Estate tax, they call it nowadays, but we must be realistic. I'm dying, whatever the doctors may say and death doesn't frighten me. Seen too much of it to care, and you'll be the boss of the firm before a week's out.

"You already are on paper, actually, though you never guessed it. Just imagined you were signing a dividend slip, but that signature and mine gives you full control, which is what I want to talk about." Vale left the porthole and sat down on the edge of his bunk.

"Blood may be thicker than water, but its not half as thick as thieves, and there'll be only two thieves you can trust before long. Peter Kent and Billy Mackenzie will teach you the business and you'll listen to them and learn the trade. Hard work, but you'll soon start to enjoy it, because you're my niece, my adopted daughter and my heir.

"Sorry, heiress of course." He smiled faintly and lifted his legs up onto the bunk. "Always been a chauvinistic male pig, Janet, and I never taught you a single useful thing.

"Never let you learn, if it comes to that. 'University, Janet?' He changed his tone and mocked himself. "Why should Miss Vale need an education? She's got enough brass of her own to keep her happy.

"'Teachers training colleges – art classes and schools of domestic economy. Fiddlesticks – what use are they to Janet Vale, Sir Simon's adopted daughter?'

"Yes, always a bloody pig, Jan. Thought I knew best, but was usually wrong." His normal voice returned, though it was very weak and barely audible. "But you mustn't worry, my darling. Certainly don't fret over that damned book. Have the last copy tomorrow and then – can't hurt – either of us again." Vale's head slumped back on the pillow, his eyes closed and his lips stopped moving.

"The book, Uncle? *Men of Courage?*" Memories of what she had heard from Tom and Mott hammered Janet's brain and she was suddenly terrified. Was it possible? Could she be involved in at least four murders?

"Please, Uncle – please try to tell me. What is there about that book which can harm us?" She shook Vale's arm, but there was no response. As Willy Mackenzie had remarked, "The chief was having one of his bad turns again."

"That's the lot, Mayne." Mott laid a row of photographs on the desk. "Those are copies of the illustrations taken from *Men of Courage*, so have a squint and tell me if you see anything interesting, anything worth committing murder for?"

"No – no – no." Tom peered at the prints. There were thirty in all, and though they were mostly dramatic, he could see nothing incriminating. "But just a moment, isn't that Simon Vale, Janet's uncle?"

"It is indeed, though taken a long time ago." Mott craned over his shoulder. "Nineteen fifty-seven or eight when Sir Simon was the sole survivor of a motor accident. Old Simon was in the back seat when the car driven by his brother, Ted, hit the embankment near Barnes. Ted and his wife, Janet's parents, were thrown through the windscreen into the Thames, and in spite of cuts and bruises, Simon plunged in after 'em. A gallant but vain rescue attempt, because they were both dead and a police launch recovered the bodies an hour or two later.

"Proves that Simon deserves a place in the book though, as does the exhibit beside it." He pointed at the bows of a sinking ship and read the caption below the picture. 'The last moments of the frigate, *River Madoc*, photographed from *Sam and Helen's* lifeboat, shortly before the start of her epic voyage.'

"Yes, old Sir Simon Vale is an extremely brave man, Mayne, but where has it got him? Just a step on his road to dusty death?

"Anything else which might seem significant?"

"Not a thing." Tom had come to the end of the collection and he looked up. "But you – you've got an idea, Mr Mott, and I'd like to hear it."

"Oh no, not yet." Mott shook his head ponderously. "I've already suspected one innocent man unjustly and I'm not making accusations against what may be a perfectly respectable group of people. But I've got an idea – a theory – and I hope to Christ I am wrong.

"Your lucky escape the other night gave me the notion, son, but let me be mistaken. Pray that J. Molden-Mott is just a stupid, credulous fool, because if I'm right, this joker didn't just kill for books. He wanted money and power and love – such a lot of all three possessions." Mott paused and started to refill his pipe again. "Must be wrong – have to be, though we'll know tomorrow, Mayne, so wait till then.

"You see, if I'm not a fool and I don't think I am –" A match to the bowl, smoke to the ceiling and a lowering of the voice. "If I'm right, Little Miss Vale will be in trouble – dead trouble!"

Thirteen

"Yes, a motor accident which took place in September 1957 or '58, Mr Mott. That is quite some time ago, but I remember the incident fairly well, as I was attached to Barnes when it happened." Mott had finally pocketed his pride and contacted the police, and an old friend, Detective Chief Superintendent Brant, spoke to him on the telephone. "As far as I can recall, witnesses stated that the car was travelling far too fast and the driver was probably drunk, though no blood test was made of course. Very lax, we were in those days." The superintendent paused to clear his throat. "However accidents can happen and they frequently do, more's the pity, and no blame can be attached to Sir Simon Vale. He acted most heroically in fact, and I was proud to shake him by the hand afterwards.

"No, speed and alcohol just don't go together and I'd step up the penalties accordingly. That is probably what happened in Miss Vale's case and she and Mr Mayne had an exceptionally lucky escape.

"A book – my book, Mr Mott. You've read the manuscript already?" Brant's spirits rose, but they were soon deflated. "Oh, a work called *Men of Courage*, which is up for sale at Foden's tomorrow.

"I know nothing about that, so please fill me in." He listened to the story and made a note in his jotting pad. "Not really our affair without definite evidence, though I wish you the best of luck, of course.

"But, Mr Mott, don't – please don't start suspecting Sir Simon Vale of anything dishonest. He may be ill, he may talk strangely, but he's just about the finest Englishman I've ever known.

"Very nice to have spoken to you, and goodbye for the present. Let's meet before too long." Brant replaced the receiver, but his fingers still hovered over the cardboard cover. The super had literary ambitions, though he hadn't decided on a title as yet. *My Fight against Crime* might appeal to the serious, but *Life as a Rozzer* had a popular ring. Mott already had the script and if he read it he might try to find him a publisher, but there were other individuals to be considered.

"The finest Englishman I've ever met." That might be true and Vale certainly had an interest in three publishing firms, but what about Superintendent Brant's own future?

Super was not a bad rank to retire at, but chief constable or commissioner would be far better. Beside, he'd given the man his word, and the man was a dangerous man to trifle with.

Very dangerous! For just over two minutes, Brant considered his course of action and then he lifted the telephone again and dialled a number. A further minute passed before a crippled hand picked up another instrument and a voice answered him.

"Thank you, Mr Brant. Thank you very much indeed and you won't find me ungenerous." Two fingers lowered a receiver onto its rest and their owner smiled. "A long, long time, Sergeant," he said. "But if all goes well, we should be almost home and dry at last." He paused and thought about the trail he had followed for over thirty years, and the men and women who had guided him on the way.

A clerk at a government office – a friend at a foreign embassy. A high-ranking officer and a Scotland Yard commander. Inspector Pounder, Superintendent Brant, Mr Mott and Thomas Mayne. He hardly knew Tom Mayne, but all those people had helped and with any luck revenge would be sweet.

"The Book of the Dead, Sergeant," he said. "That's what I called the volume and tomorrow I should see it. The Foden Gallery at about three o'clock tomorrow afternoon." He still smiled, but there was no mirth or good humour in his expression. His face looked as if a gargoyle was grinning. "See the book, or see the person who tries to buy it. Doesn't really matter which. All I want is revenge, and that's supposed to be sweet."

"A first, ladies and gentlemen. Lot 25 must surely be one of the rarest and most sought-after books in the world." Mr Gordon Glover nodded to a porter who held up a slim, faded volume for the audience's benefit. "You are looking at an authentic first edition of *Alice's Adventures in Wonderland*, or *Alice Underground* as Dr Dodgson (Lewis Carroll) originally called it." Glover cleared his throat and wished that the cover wasn't so faded, the binding so loose and the interior so grimy. "I realize of course that this specimen can hardly be described as '*fine*' but it bears the signature, C.L. Dodgson, on the flyleaf and all the pages are intact. What may I start at please?

"Thank you, Mr Latimer. I have three thousand pounds, which is a very modest sum indeed for such an item. Mrs Budd – four. Mr Latimer – four and a half.

"Any advance on four and a half, ladies and gentlemen? Ah, thank you, Doctor." A valued customer at the back of the room spread out his fingers, and Glover banged down the hammer quickly. "Sold to Dr Howard Gotlieb of Boston University Libraries for five thousand pounds sterling." Not really a bad price, he thought. Alice might be rare, she might be signed, but it would take the Libraries' Restoration Department a long time to make her look presentable.

"And now for a novelty, my friends." He watched the porter raise a thick wad of yellow papers. "Lot 26 is the supposed diary of Heinrich Himmler, compiled during the last three years before the poor – " Glover had been about to say, "before the poor man committed suicide," but checked himself in time.

" – before this poor vile wretch took his own life by swallowing cyanide to avoid retribution in May, 1945.

"A coward's way out, and we at Foden Gallery make no claim that the manuscript is genuine of course, though it was discovered in a ruined building near Flensburg; Himmler's last official headquarters in Northern Germany."

"Get on, man." "Sell that pile of rubbish." "Put up the last lot and show the truth." "Whoever is hurt, I've got to face it." At the right hand side of the room, Tom and Mott and Janet waited impatiently. As soon as Himmler was disposed of, *Men of Courage* would be offered for sale and the murderer might reveal himself.

They looked forward to that revelation with varied feelings, and Tom's were mixed. He didn't know exactly what Molden-Mott's theory might be, but he suspected. If those suspicions were proved correct, someone he had grown very fond of was going to be badly hurt and he didn't want Janet to be hurt – he didn't want that at all.

Janet's emotions consisted of dumb misery and acceptance. She had no idea what secret the book contained, but she was almost certain that her family had been involved in some scandal. She wanted to know the truth, but the truth terrified her. A car which *happened* to crash, Simon Vale had said that in the *Bully Boy's* cabin. Uncle had never cared for her parents and he admitted his dislike openly. Did the crash just *happen*, or had he arranged it?

Mott, on the other hand, appeared totally unconcerned. Like a decadent Roman emperor, he leaned on his stick and waited for the Christians to enter the arena, and watch the real fun begin. In a very few minutes, Glover would offer the book for sale and a mass murderer must show his hand. If only Glover would stop talking and get on with his job. He listened to the man's fruity voice and tapped the floor impatiently with his ferrule.

"No, we of the Foden make no claim that these diaries were actually written by Himmler himself, though the handwriting and the paper both tally. And even if they are forgeries, the forger apparently knew Reichführer Himmler personally. There is a most interesting account of his relationship with Adolf Eichmann. The implications are quite Freudian." Glover paused and chuckled, "What can we start at?

"One pound!" A small bespectacled man had raised a

single finger and the mirth ceased. "I'm afraid you must be joking, sir. We do not accept bids of under ten pounds at the Foden.

"Ah, one thousand pounds. That is more accurate." The bidder had corrected his mistake and Glover's frown faded. "I have one thousand, so do I hear any advance on that figure?

"No, then sold to Mr ..." He appealed to the purchaser for help. "I'm afraid, I do not know your name, or address, sir. Thank you. Sold to Herr Stinkentroüser of Garmish-Partenkirchen for the sum of one thousand pounds."

"Not Stinkentroüser – Steinehauser." The German protested, but Mott hardly heard him. The big moment was approaching and he stared around the room while Glover consulted his catalogue. With any luck, he might spot the suspect before the bidding opened.

But what was wrong – what was happening? Why was no porter holding up his copy of *Men of Courage*? Why didn't Glover call out the lot number? Why had he risen to his feet, taken a sip of water and smiled?

"Well, my friends. I'm afraid that that concludes our business for the present," he said. "All that remains is for me to thank you for your amicable co-operation and hope that we shall meet again shortly. The practice of holding book sales on Thursday afternoons has become quite a feature of Foden's recently and I'm sure you will agree that it has been a most satisfactory arrangement.

"I beg your pardon, Fred." His clerk had whispered to him and leaned forward. "Ah yes, and you were quite right to remind me.

"Ladies and gentlemen." He cleared his throat and spoke as blandly as before. "The final lot advertised in our catalogue, which is a Raeburn Press limited edition of a book entitled *Men of Courage*, was withdrawn by its owner, shortly before the sale opened. I sincerely hope that this has caused no one any disappointment or inconvenience, but the proprietor's wishes must always be observed."

"What the devil!" Mott gave a hollow groan and his hand gripped Tom's arm like a vice. "Did you tell Glover to withdraw the copy, Mayne, and if not, what went wrong?"

"Of course I didn't tell him anything of the kind." Tom was almost as astounded as Mott by the announcement. "You handed me the book at eleven o'clock and I delivered it to Glover at half-past with our written instructions." Tom pulled his arm free. "There can only be one explanation. Someone bribed Glover and got at him first."

"Yes, that seems likely, and Mr Gordon Glover is going to have a lesson he won't forget in a hurry. Come on, Mayne. Out of the way, sir. Let me pass, madam." Mott grasped the end of his stick and strode forward with Tom at his heels. He elbowed aside everyone who blocked their way and reached the dais just as Glover was about to step down.

"Now, Mr Glover, just what explanation have you to offer?" Mott mounted the steps and his face glowed like a great, scarlet ball of indignation. "I happen to be the owner of that book and I gave no orders for its withdrawal, so answer me."

"I don't understand." For a moment Glover responded bravely enough. A bishop defying the pagan hoards from his altar and then he asked a question which was to be his undoing. "Is your friend a lunatic, Mr Mayne?"

"A lunatic!" Mott's fury increased. "You dare call me that, you murderer, accessory, Iscariot." His stick swung out and caught the auctioneer's kneecap. Glover screamed and then bolted for his door like a panic-stricken black rabbit, but he did not get far. The handle of the stick seemed to leap forward and encircle his neck and he fell to the floor with a crash that shook the room.

From her place by the wall, Janet watched the tumult, as though it was a scene from some early slapstick comedy. Three porters had hurled themselves on Mott in an attempt to drag him back and the public were starting to panic. She just stared fascinated till a hand clutched her arm.

"Let's get out of this beargarden, Miss Janet." The voice at her side sounded worried and sad. "I've brought bad news, I'm afraid; the worst news of all. The chief is dead and it's time you faced the truth at last," said Peter Kent.

"I certainly intend to prefer charges, Sergeant. I have been outraged, humiliated and physically injured." Glover lay on a sofa in his office and he no longer looked urbane or pompous. His coat was torn, his right eye was starting to swell and there was a long graze down one side of his face. His breath came in gasps and he resembled a huge dying fish that has been too long out of water.

"This young man instructed me to sell an almost valueless book and put a reserve on the price at two thousand pounds." He pointed a shaky finger at Tom. "Well, that's what I got for it, Mayne. The cash is in my safe, and our commission will be used to cover the costs of this hooligan's trial." He stared at Mott with a mixture of dread and indignation. "And the assault took place in public too ∟ in the gallery itself – before the very eyes of my audience." He raised his hand to rub a tear from his own swollen eye. "The shame, disgrace and humiliation! Never be able to hold up my head again."

"Why, you puffed-up nonentity!" Mott appeared to be about to attack again, but the presence of three policemen deterred him. "Your reputation no longer exists, Mr Gordon Glover, and we want to know what happened to that book. My book, which was entrusted to you to offer for public auction." His fist thumped a table to drive home the point. "Well, what became of it? Who did you sell the copy to?"

"I was about to tell you, if you'd only give me the chance. I did sell it. About half an hour before the sale opened a man came in here and said that he wished to buy *Men of Courage* privately. We never do business like that usually of course, but when I told him the reserve Mayne had placed on the thing, he opened his brief-case and produced a stack of twenty-pound notes. I counted them of course, and checked the serial numbers for duplicates. All quite genuine, and two thousand pounds in cash. Thought you'd have been pleased, Mayne, but instead you bring a hired bully along to assault me."

"Normally I would have been pleased, Mr Glover; very pleased." Tom leaned against a wall feeling utter weariness and defeat. They had lost. That must have been about the last copy of the book in existence and the killer had got away with it, as he had with all the others. "But do you know the man, Mr Glover?" Even as he asked the question Tom realized it was useless. "Did he give you a name or an address?"

"No, never seen him, till today. Told me his name was Smith, though that seemed unlikely. Said he was the agent of a rich collector who didn't mind what he paid, but hated the publicity of public auctions.

"But surely, you know him, Mayne? Yes, he was sitting behind that young lady you were with. Couldn't take his eyes off her, and just before –" Once again, fear and anger crossed Glover's face. " – before that cowardly assault, I saw him lean forward as if he was about to touch her."

"That young lady!" Click – click – click. Like a jigsaw puzzle, the pieces were fitting together in Tom's brain, and a picture had started to emerge.

Janet – Janet Vale, she was the key to the door, but where was Janet? They'd left her in the sale-room, but that was almost half an hour ago. She had been approached by an anonymous buyer who called himself Smith and . . .

Ignoring Mott's bellow of protest, Tom started to hurry out of the office, but a large, military figure blocked his way.

"Ah, you're Mayne, ain't yer? Got a shop in Chelsea. Been there a couple of times, but never found anything worth buying. Came away with a load of dust on me hands." The man had a flowing white moustache and a cigar jutted between his lips. "Not on business today, so you can relax and stand at ease, Sergeant Dawson." He grinned at the policeman who had come to attention. "Had enough trouble with petty officialdom already, as your chap outside didn't even know who I was. Hate throwing weight about, but I had to mention the Chief Commissioner and a few other good pals at the Yard before he'd let me through.

"Well, Mr Mott. Hail to thee, blithe spirit, and I trust you've managed to make a mess of Friend Glover." He eyed the recumbent figure on the couch and chuckled. "Yes, I see you have, and please accept my heartiest congratulations. Never liked the toad, and always wanted a copy of Willie Maugham's *Painted Veil*. The proper edition that is, with the Hong Kong libel passages intact. The Foden had one a few months ago, but I missed it. Mr Glover didn't even bother to send me a catalogue.

"Yes, revenge is sweet, Mr Mott, but even if I'm not the actual avenger myself, I'm curious to know your motives. Why – what provoked you to attack a seemingly honest citizen."

"I'll tell you, General Kirk. I'll tell you all I do know, though it's not very much at the moment." Mott started to do so, using the personal pronoun freely, but Kirk suddenly checked him and raised a hand for silence. A torn talon of a hand with three fingers lopped off at the joints. "Yes, very little, Mr Molden-Mott. That girl who came with you – Janet Vale. She left with a man and you don't even know his name.

"Well, I do, or should. As a former chief of the Intelligence Service, I need to know damn near everything, so where have I seen that feller before?

"God, you keep a cold dump in here." He tightened his jacket with the two remaining right-hand fingers and glared at Glover. "Too chilly to concentrate, but let me think.

"Yes, he spoke to Janet Vale, and she just followed him out of the room and missed half the fun. Never believed women have much in the top storey meself, but she seemed concerned about some relative who was dead or dying." He tapped his forehead with the horrible maimed hand.

"Though that doesn't answer my question. Who was the man with her? Seen his picture somewhere. In one of the financial papers, I think, but he didn't look like a financier.

Looked like a run-of-the-mill NCO type. Sergeant, corporal, petty officer; something along those lines, though he wouldn't be much use as a fighting man today. Far too long in the tooth, if he has any teeth of his own left, which I doubt.

"Shut up, Mayne. I'm getting warmer." He removed the cigar from his lips and pointed it at Tom like a pistol. "Somerset, Yorkshire, Cumbria – some such county name, but not one of those.

"Lancashire – Devonshire – Kent. Got it!" Kirk's whole expression changed and he suddenly seemed twenty years younger. "Yes, the chap is called Kent, of course. Peter Kent and he was one of old Vale's original partners at A.C.E. Also a survivor of that blasted tug which went for a burton in 1944." Not only Kirk's expression had changed, but his whole face altered. His features looked as hard as lava setting into granite.

"It fits, gentlemen. It really does fit at last, because Sir Simon has had a second stroke. He must be the relative that Kent referred to. Simon Vale is dead and he left Janet a legacy.

"Well, what are you waiting for, Mr Mott? I've got a vehicle outside, and there's no time to shilly-shally about here. The Vales have a ruddy great mansion in Hampstead, a house in Sussex, and Janet owns a flat near Kensington.

"The Sussex place is called Inver Lodge, outside Brighton, so telephone the locals at once, Sergeant, tell them to pick up Kent right away, under any pretext, and we'll attend to the Hampstead mausoleum.

"What's that, Mayne? You say that they won't be at either address, but on a launch moored above Richmond, the *Bully Boy*.

"Yes, that might fit, and I hope you're right. Been interested in the *Bully* for years, but never managed to nail her." He was already hurrying towards the exit with Tom and Mott following. "Is Miss Janet in any real danger, Mayne? Don't know – haven't a clue, but I'll give you a quotation, from another book:

"As our mother the frigate, bepainted and fine,
Did work for her Bully, the ship of the line."

"Question of character, really. Will Janet Vale accept the *Bully's* gifts and her uncle's fortune?"

Simon Vale was dead, there was no doubt about that. His body lay in the cabin beneath Janet's feet and he looked small and innocent. A wax dummy which had never really been alive.

"Yes, the demon's name was once the Revd David Glyde, though he's in hell now and I helped to put him there." Kent pulled a book out of his jacket and flicked through the pages. "No regrets or self-incrimination, miss, though I don't deny that Mr Glyde was a clever man. Not self-seeking and not after money. All he wanted was power – the means to make people squirm, and he found it; here."

He held out the book, open at a photograph which Janet recognized, though it meant hardly anything to her.

"But that's the frigate, *River Madoc*, sinking just before the *Sam* followed her off the North Cape. My uncle took the photograph from the lifeboat at the start of your journey home."

"At the end of the voyage, Miss Janet, and not from a lifeboat." Kent still spoke without any emotion. "No lifeboat was required and the *Sam* had only two, and one went off to look for the *Madoc's* survivors. The crew never came back, and the *Sam* was never torpedoed. We lost the lads in the fog and they vanished under five thousand feet of water.

"Only four of us were left on board the *Sam*, and there's one of 'em, miss." He pointed towards Mackenzie at the *Bully's* wheel. "Four men aren't really enough to sail a largish ship, but we did it. The chief insisted we took her home and there were no complaints, though he worked us stupid.

"No complaints when he took and published that damned picture later, though we never suspected the Devil might see that the *Madoc* was phoney.

"Approved at the time. Thought it was a good idea at the

time. A sort of smoke screen to conceal the truth, but Glyde rumbled us. The revd gentleman studied that photograph and saw what it really was.

"Not the bows of a sinking warship, Miss Janet, but the tip of a ruddy rock in Scotland."

Kirk's vehicle, as he called it, was a large German staff car built by Mercedes around 1940 and acquired by its present owner during some long-forgotten skirmish. The general's driver was equally large and archaic. A gross, fat man who answered to the name of Sergeant David Drudge and had served his master in war and peace for many years.

"Come on, Drudge," Kirk bellowed as soon as he and Tom and Mott had clambered into the back seat. "Start her up and let's get cracking. Turn left at the first traffic lights, and then along the embankment."

"First left, sir." The horrible car shuddered as Dodge let out the clutch. "But then, which way along, General? The embankment runs both east and west."

"West, you fool, and stop dawdling. We're off to Richmond, so get your foot down on the accelerator, and keep it there. Could be a matter of life or death if we're late." The speed increased slightly and Kirk turned to his companions in the back. "Drudge really is a huge, fat, idle fellow, Mr Mott. Impertinent too. Don't know why I keep him on. Charity perhaps – kindness of heart, maybe."

"Why did you use the expression 'life or death', General Kirk?" The word "charity" reminded Tom of what Janet had said in the shop after buying Mrs Rayner's worthless collection. "Is Miss Vale in danger?"

"Possibly, Mayne, but it depends on her attitude and her conscience. Sir Simon is dead. Janet is on board the *Bully Boy* and at least four other people died because of that book; *Men of Courage*." Kirk tossed his cigar stub out of a window and frowned. "Not sure why they were killed, Mr Mott, but I've got a hunch, and my hunches are liable to hit pay dirt.

"Let's consider the facts and go back to the beginning – to 1944." They had reached the embankment at last and he watched the river flowing alongside. "At the beginning of Hitler's war, a thousand-ton salvage tug, the *Sam and Helen*, was commandeered into the navy for use as a rescue vessel and most of her original crew stayed with her.

"Can't blame the blighters for that. Those merchant navy wallahs got double danger money for special duties. The only RN personnel on the *Sam* were six D.E.M.S., gunners commanded by a lieutenant: Simon Vale.

"Well, by all accounts, the *Sam* didn't have too bad a time, till the winter of 1943, when she was sent off to North Russia. Heavy seas, constant darkness and enemy air attacks took a heavy toll, but she reached Murmansk, though with a sadly depleted complement.

"And she stayed there, that's the first interesting thing. The *Sam* had suffered loss of life, but was perfectly seaworthy, yet she rotted off harbour for almost a year. And, at a time when convoys were desperate for every bit of help they could get, so any ideas why, gentlemen?" He looked at Tom and Mott but they both shook their heads.

"No, though you should be able to imagine the conditions aboard the *Sam* after such a period. Almost a full year off a bleak Russian coast with no booze, no women and no shore leave. Wonder that there wasn't a mutiny, but two factors may have stopped that. The master and Lieutenant Vale were strict disciplinarians and they could have told some of the crew what to wait for.

"Well, the waiting finally ended and the frigate *River Madoc* arrived, with orders to escort the *Sam* home. Another *why*, gentlemen. Why should the British Admiralty have sent a new and valuable frigate, just out of the builders' hands, to escort a miserable little old-fashioned tug back to Scotland?"

"Edinburgh, Mayne." For no reason he could think of, Tom muttered the city's name and Kirk nodded. "Yes, you're getting slightly warmer, though H.M.S. *Edinburgh* was sunk in the Barents Sea much earlier and the *Sam* and the *Madoc* had rounded the North Cape before disaster struck.

"Will you stop idling, Sergeant?" Kirk bellowed at Drudge who had slowed to avoid a taxi. "No time to lose. Still a long way to journey's end, so get on faster.

"Not many German submarines around by that time, and we never learned the U-boat's number or where she came from, but she blasted the *Madoc* with a torpedo that sent her down in just about a thousand fathoms.

"I know that Lieutenant Vale (Sir Simon, as he was, till recently) was supposed to have photographed the frigate sinking, Mr Mott." Kirk frowned at the interruption. "But what did the picture show and where was it taken from? A lifeboat or a tugboat and . . .

"Oh, my God!" The general gasped as though he had received a blow in the stomach. "We're too late and there she is. Faster, far faster than I imagined, so don't blame me if we have a prang." The tyres screamed as Drudge swung the wheel hard over and Tom saw the object which had caused Kirk's consternation. A long, grey shape had appeared round a bend of the Thames. All grey, apart from a name at its bows, the water creaming under the bows, and a red ensign flowing at the stern. The *Bully Boy* was fast, as Kirk had said. Much faster than any normal river craft, and she was passing them before Drudge had completed his turn. "Good show, Sergeant, but we must overhaul her before the Tower Bridge, and you two listen to me." Kirk looked at Tom and Mott through angry bloodshot eyes. "I take it that you re a fit man, Mr Mott, and you're a young man, Mayne. Certainly younger and fitter than Drudge and I, so here are your instructions. Providing we get to the bridge before that damned launch, you must jump off the parapet and board her."

Fourteen

"No, Miss Janet, the frigate caught a tin fish, but the *Sam* was never torpedoed and she didn't go down." Peter Kent leaned over the *Bully Boy's* rail and spat into the water. "Not anywhere near the North Cape that is. We scuttled her off Scotland."

"I still don't understand you, Peter." Though thin mist covered both sides of the river, Janet could just see the dome of Saint Paul's as the *Bully Boy* moved on towards the estuary. Could just make out the Tower of London and television masts on the Surrey hills. "Why – what really happened?"

"A difficult question, miss, but I'll try to give you an answer. I suppose greed, lust and boredom were a few of the explanations, but there was also possession. I can't really talk about that, though the chief might if he was still alive; God rest him.

"Let's think of the Devil as David Glyde; he provided the temptation. Only a naval padre sent to Murmansk to attend to the sick and dying, but they gave him other duties. Super-cargo, docking superintendent, liaison officer with the Soviet authorities. What do titles matter?" Kent's voice grew bitter. "The lads on the *Sam* were damned near on the point of mutiny, when the tempter came aboard and he tempted us. Told the chief why we were lying off bloody Murmansk, and what our next cargo was to be if the Russkis kept their word.

"Gold, miss. Repayment for all the war materials we'd given the Red bastards and that's why we needed the *Madoc* as an escort. The chief repeated Glyde's information word for word and the lads listened and became quiet, though I never really understood why.

"What is there about gold that's so fascinating? You can't do nothing with the stuff, except make ornaments, and what real use are they, Miss Janet? But, the whole crew were aquiver when the boxes came aboard, and so was I. We all imagined those cases were our own property and they turned out to be after the *Madoc* bought it.

"Your uncle tried to stop 'em launching a boat to look for survivors, but the skipper insisted. 'Flesh and blood, and Jackie Tars stand together'. Those were the fool's actual words, and he set off with a dozen other fools for company. Off into the mist, and that was the last we saw of 'em." Kent's voice had grown strident and Janet sensed he was not quite sane. "Only four of us were left on board and the mist was thickening into dense fog. No time to wait for the lifeboat to come back and the chief gave Mac his orders." He nodded at Mackenzie who was crouched over the wheel. 'You're supposed to be an engineer, man, so what's delaying you? Start the diesels and we'll get the hell out of here. We're on our way home, lads. Home to Bonnie Scotland in the morning'.

"Well, we got home, though twenty-two mornings passed before we sighted the British coast. The *Sam* was a pretty fast vessel. She could raise fifteen knots at a pinch, but there was to be no record breaking on that trip. We crawled through the fog blind, and praying that no other ships might spot us and ask questions. But at last we smelled the land and knew that our long journey was over."

"And so you scuttled the *Sam* in shallow water and came ashore in the second lifeboat." Janet thought she knew almost everything now. Everything, except the one thing that mattered. "How long before you returned to collect the cargo, Peter?"

"About nine months, Miss Janet, given a day or two either way." Kent looked at the gleaming deck of the launch and grinned. "We bought the *Bully* on credit and spent some time fitting her up. We had a long way to go, you see, because a private individual can't hold gold in England.

"We weren't private individuals then of course. We'd all decided what to do with the money and drawn up contracts, accordingly.

"Finding the *Sam* was no trouble because the chief had

made sure of that. She lay under a rock called the Hag of Skulda in less than fifty feet of water, but getting the gold out was a bit of a sweat. Ten cases we raised and each case held twenty-eight pounds of the stuff.

"Not nearly as much as that cruiser, H.M.S. *Edinburgh*, they salvaged not so long ago, carried, Miss Janet, but a hell of a lot of money, three hundred US dollars an ounce it fetched in Tangiers and we were rich.

"Rich enough to start A.C.E. and, owing to the chief, the business grew. Not merely chemicals today, Miss Janet. Shipping and textiles, an airline and three civil engineering firms. Fun it was – rather like playing Monopoly, until . . ."

"Until what, Peter?" He had paused and Janet prompted him. "What spoiled your money game?"

"This – this damned book, Miss Janet. And the Devil of course. The Revd Mr Glyde moved to Scotland and he recognized the illustration. Not the bows of the *Madoc* sinking, but the old Hag of Skulda.

"I'll always remember the chief's face when he got Glyde's letter, though it wasn't a blackmail note in the financial sense of the word. The Devil doesn't want money, but needs power – the power to hurt and make people squirm." Kent's own face seemed to shrivel as he stared at the picture. "No signature and though the envelope was marked private, it had a Scottish postmark.

"I won't tell you what the message read, Miss Janet. It was obscene and vile and every word stank of evil. The Bent One had the chief in the hollow of his hand and intended to squeeze the soul out of him.

"Squeeze slowly, but we were quicker eh, Mac?" He raised his voice and Mackenzie nodded. "Hired killers do exist if you can pay 'em and we could pay the best. We traced Glyde through his publishers, the Church Commissioners, and the Admiralty filled us in on his war record.

"Our man found Glyde in Scotland and made him talk before he died, though I won't go into details

"And don't worry, Miss Janet. There's nothing to worry about." He looked at her with deep concern. "Professional assassins have a code of ethics like doctors and lawyers and our murderer was perfectly satisfied with his fee. At the moment he's probably spending it in South America and he won't talk."

"And Pike, and the old man at the publishers." Janet felt sickened and not only by Kent's confession – her own blood was to blame. "Were they liquidated too?"

"Oh, yes, Miss Janet, and you must understand why. Though Glyde was out of the way, the book itself remained a threat and a chap called Kirk came on the scene. General Charles Kirk is a retired intelligence officer and a pal at the Admiralty told him about the *Sam's* gold.

"Don't suppose Kirk could discover anything sinister, but he questioned the chief some years ago and we don't take chances; not where the firm's concerned." The launch was sliding under Waterloo Bridge and Kent spoke louder to make himself heard. "We decided to buy up every copy of the book and Pike was an obvious agent, but he started to ask outrageous prices. Either he'd become greedy or had stumbled on the truth. He had to die.

"No regrets about Messrs Pike or Glyde, though I'm sorry about that old clerk at the publishers and I was desperately saddened by what almost happened to you the other night, Miss Janet. Only recognized you at the last moment and just pulled aside in time."

"You! Peter!" Janet remembered the incident. She and Tom, strolling towards the pub, a car mounting the pavement under the flyover and hurtling towards them. "You were at the wheel of that car?"

"Yes, but you must believe me. When you told your uncle about Mayne's interest in the book, he decided that Mayne had to go and I was appointed to be the executioner.

"Please forgive me, Miss Janet. Just thought you were some friend of Mayne's or his shop assistant, perhaps. Only missed you by inches, and you must believe this." Kent lowered his head and he looked like a dog. A faithful, devoted dog begging to be pardoned for some misdeed. "If I'd harmed you, I think I'd have killed myself."

"I believe you, Peter, but what about Tom Mayne?" Janet stared at the bowed head with something very close to compassion. "Is he still on the executioner's death list?"

"Not unless you want him to die, Miss Janet, and there's no valid reason that I can see." Kent closed the book and held it over the rail. "What harm can Mayne, or anyone else, do without evidence, and this is all the evidence. The last existing copy of *Men of Courage* and soon it will be buried under Thames mud.

"Only three things to do now, miss. Dispose of the book. Give the chief his Viking funeral and then ..." He raised his eyes and stared at her. *"Le Roi est Mort – Vive la Reine."*

"Well, here we are at last and about time too." The Mercedes had stopped on the middle of Tower Bridge and Kirk climbed out and peered upstream. "No sign of the blighters yet, so they've either given us the slip or are on their way.

"And you ... What the hell are you thinking of, man?" A chorus of horns and human abuse made him swing round and glower at Drudge. "You're holding up the traffic and causing an obstruction, Sergeant, so don't just sit there like a ruddy dowager. Get off your rump, wave 'em on and open the bonnet. If you peer at her innards pathetically, people might just think you've broken down and feel sorry for you.

"God, that stupid fellow makes me furious, gentlemen." The pandemonium had stopped and he rejoined Tom and Mott at the paraphet. "Though not as furious as the suspicion that our birds have flown."

"Have they, General?" Tom was also looking up the Thames. "Isn't that the launch now; just passing Canon Street?"

"Could be – might be." Kirk raised a hand to his forehead. "Eyes not so good these days, but what do you think, Mr Mott?"

"I'm not certain yet." Mott studied a grey shape approach-ing the next bridge upstream. "Yes, that's the *Bully Boy* all right. About three-quarters of a mile away and coming along fast. She's keeping well over to port at present, and if that course is maintained we should meet her at the inner arch." He squared his shoulders before marching forwards. "Ready, Mayne, and don't worry. Feel no anxiety on my account. I may have been crippled in Scotland, I may look slightly ill, but there is noth-ing wrong with my heart. An Englishman's heart beats for England, and together we shall strike a great blow for the old country and the world will ring with our fame."

"England! What a pompous boor that fellow is," Kirk thought as he followed them. "England could only lose by Molden-Mott's great blow for the old country. Factories would have to close, workers be laid off and exports diminish. Also a dead man's reputation might be tarnished and stripped of all honour.

"But why, Charlie Kirk? You gave Mott his instructions and he will jump because you put the idea into his thick skull. Why – why did you have to start a crusade against Simon Vale and his empire?"

Justice – righteousness – truth? The search for truth cer-tainly came into it, but there were other far more important reasons. Revenge – retaliation – a vendetta, were the key words.

He had known that the tugboat *Sam* was laden with gold at Murmansk. A midshipman on the *Madoc* had told him so. The boy had written his parents a long, chatty letter. Enquir-ies about their health, news about the crew, the account of a novel he had been reading. Nothing that a censor could possi-bly object to, but if you substituted the second and third letter of every other word with an agreed numeral, you had a code. A simple personal cipher which he and Allan had worked out together, long before the boy joined the navy.

Allan was only 17 when he'd written that note. A smart boy for his age, though he died within a week of composing it. Allan had met Vale, the *Sam's* gunnery officer, and seen through him. The private message read. "V – mad. If hit – no survivors will be picked up."

Kirk still kept that faded sheet of paper, and he often looked at the end, which was entirely innocent. "Your very loving son – Allan Kirk."

That had been the start of Kirk's enquiry and it had taken him almost forty years to be sure. He watched Mott and Tom station themselves against the parapet of the bridge and prayed for revenge.

Nearly half a century, prying and probing into the affairs of Simon Vale and A.C.E., and soon he might have proof. A little book to expose murder.

Fifteen

"You left those men to freeze or drown in that cold northern water; for gold?" Janet stared at Kent leaning against the rail and she felt no revulsion; only pity. "Why, Peter? Just a few cases of yellow metal. You told me yourself, that gold is virtually worthless and you must give me a reason."

"The metal itself had no real value, but it's what you can buy with the stuff which counts. The chief – your uncle kept explaining that, and events proved him right." Kent looked like an uncertain crusader, attempting to justify his cause. "We bought power, Miss Janet. Not only stocks and shares and money in the bank, but an empire. A great kingdom, and the chief has willed it all to you.

"Yes, to you, Miss Janet. You're the boss of A.C.E. now. You'll sit in the boardroom and deliver orders, and I'll stand at your side and see that there aren't any mistakes. There could be a few at first, but not many. You're the chief's own flesh and blood and you'll soon learn how to control underlings."

"Power" – "control" – "underlings". The words made Janet think of a passage from the Gospels. "The Devil taketh Him up unto an exceedingly high mountain and showeth Him all the kingdoms of the world and the glory of them."

No, that quotation didn't really apply. Peter Kent wasn't the tempter. He'd fallen into temptation. Peter was just a loyal subordinate who enjoyed obeying orders, providing he respected the person who delivered them. Satan lay in the cabin below, and he had once been called Sir Simon Vale.

And the offer was not really a temptation to her. Board meetings and balance sheets and endless conferences. The constant knowledge that she was living on stolen money and the lives of the dead. The prospect was appalling, and she tried to speak like her uncle and held out a hand. "The book,

Peter. Give me that book. I wish to show it to the police."

"What! I'm sorry, miss, but I don't understand." For a second, Kent frowned and then he smiled and turned to Mackenzie who was steering towards the left arch of Tower Bridge. "Did you hear that, Mac? Send it along to Scotland Yard with the illustration ripped out, of course; very funny? That will puzzle our brave boys in blue and tell 'em nothing. Just the kind of thing the chief might have thought of, and you're a chip off the old block, all right, miss."

"I'm not joking, Peter, and that book must go to Scotland Yard with the evidence intact." Janet stared at his eyes and she spoke very slowly. "I never wanted control of the firm, you see, and I can't accept it now, though I don't imagine you'll go to prison. Your hired killer won't talk and the *Madoc* sank years ago. A good barrister will show that you and Mac were just ratings, obeying their officer's orders, and didn't understand the consequences."

"You honestly think that that's important. That my life and Mackenzie's matter? Well, you're wrong, Miss Janet – terribly wrong." He stared at her with complete conviction. "The average human being isn't worth a damn, and death has no meaning, the only significant thing is the *Geist* – The will to create and conquer. I know that's true, miss. The chief said it long ago 'Open the door when opportunity knocks' was one of his favourite maxims."

"Then my uncle contaminated you, Peter." Janet stared at him and she tried not to shudder. Peter Kent's face was not merely altering, he was growing younger. His middle-aged features had lost their wrinkles and a boy's face was watching her. By some trick of light or shadow, his dark city suit had become a uniform and his eyes were angry. The boy had heard his idol insulted and he would repay.

"Contaminated, Janet!" he said and for the first time, the mistress-servant relationship vanished, and he did not use the formal 'miss'. "Contaminated and corrupted by the best and noblest man who ever lived. Sir Simon offered you everything, Janet Vale, but you rejected his offer, though I wonder why.

"Oh, no my girl, don't try that." Her hand had shot out to grab the book from him, but the boy moved away quickly. "Yes, I do know why you hate money and power and authority, and there's only one possible reason." With the book behind his back, he studied her through his Peter Pan eyes, which would never grow old.

"You're not Janet Vale, but an impostor – a ruddy by-blow. I remember your parents: father a weakling and mother a tart. Madelaine, the Mare, the chief used to call her and as always he was right. Mummy would lift up her skirt for a dog, if he barked politely and not because of lust. Mercy and Christian charity were the Mare's motives and her daughter had better start praying to Christ right now." He tossed the book onto a hatch cover and then he came at her. His fingers round her throat, a knee in her belly and Janet went down. Down onto the deck with Kent on top of her, and she didn't struggle or cry out. She was too tired and sickened to resist Peter Kent and she also felt sorry for him.

But those weren't the only reasons for her lack of resistance. The launch was almost under Tower Bridge and from the bridge two figures were leaping towards them. With her head on the deck boards and Kent's hand throttling her Janet caught a brief glimpse of the descent, though the first figure failed to reach his target. He hit the water some six feet from the *Bully Boy's* bow, but the second man was more accurate. Tom Mayne's feet landed slap on Mackenzie's shoulders, Kent's fingers tightened and daylight went out.

"Janet – tell me that you're all right." "Of course, the girl's ok, but keep pulling, man. Do you expect me to help you with a broken arm and a fractured leg?"

The voices seemed very faint and far away, but when Janet opened her eyes, she recognized the unpleasant face of Mr Molden-Mott, and he had suffered even more damage. His other eye was blackened, his left hand clutched her ankle and his right leg trailed limply behind him. "Of course, Miss Vale's all right at the moment, but she won't be for long, and neither will I, unless you put your back into it and get us ashore."

"I'm doing my best, Mott. My very best, but how much farther have we to go?" Tom Mayne's hands were under her armpits. He was dragging her and Mott along, and the cold told her that they were in the water.

"Five – ten minutes, if you keep up the pace, so save your breath and stop us floating away downstream." Mott gasped either from pain or irritation. "'*Best!*' The young fool keeps repeating his foolishness, Miss Vale, but what really took place? I prudently leapt a few feet from the launch's bows and grabbed a line hanging over her side. I dragged myself up and suffered considerable injuries, beating off your attacker, but he ..." He raised his free hand and pointed at Tom. "Sir Galahad decided to make a direct assault. Jumped straight for the launch itself, and fell onto the helmsman. Knocked him cold and knocked out the steering gear as you can see for yourself. Try to raise your head, if that's possible, and then tell me what's about to happen."

"A collision." Janet tried to obey his orders and she saw the launch clearly. The *Bully Boy* was still travelling fast, but seemed completely out of control and was swerving towards the Pool of London. "But, the book – did either of you pick up the book?" Though Janet's throat was throbbing painfully, that was the important question. "Peter Kent threw it onto a hatch cover and one of you must have seen it."

"Didn't see a thing, except that bastard who was trying to murder you. Maniacs are supposed to have the strength of over three normal men, and he certainly proved the point. Hurled me back across the deck and might have killed us both, if young Mayne hadn't had the sense to rap his skull with a belaying-pin. Suppose I must have tripped over something of course, but it was a most miraculous escape." Mott closed his eyes, as though thanking God for the miracle. "But, get on harder, Mayne. We're not out of the woods yet. Not by a long chalk. The Viking's funeral is due to start at any moment, so pull, man – pull, as you've never pulled before."

"Ouch!" Tom responded and Janet groaned as his knee struck her spine. "Yes, my uncle wanted to be buried at sea, but so what – why the hurry?"

"Good grief! – the ignorance of young people!" Mott's thanksgiving was over and he opened his eyes and stared at her.

"A Viking's funeral wasn't just a question of dumping the chief's body overboard. The ship had to be destroyed too. Destroyed by fire, and I bet that launch has some pretty lethal explosives on board and a few detonators to trigger 'em off. That's why we didn't waste time trying to stop the engines. Had to get away quickly."

"The chief's body." Janet thought of Sir Simon Vale stretched out in the *Bully Boy's* cabin. Did Mott's words justify his actions slightly, she wondered. No, not at all. Her uncle had deserted the *Madoc's* survivors and their would-be rescuers for gain. Tom and Mott were prompted by self-preservation and Mott's next statement hinted at the truth. "You were out cold and I was only half-conscious when Mayne tossed us into the Thames. Failed to see that there was a lifeboat slung out to take those two men off when the time arose to say farewell to the big bad wolf. Bloody young fool didn't know about Norse funeral rites. Imagined that the *Bully* might collide with one of the vessels ahead and shake us up."

"And so she will." Tom's voice was hoarse from exhaustion. "Look at that Russki, Janet."

"Where, Tom?" For a moment, Janet couldn't see anything and then she heard the siren. They had floated a long way downstream and, out from the West India Docks, a ship was emerging with a tug in attendance. She flew a Union Jack at her foremast, the red Soviet ensign flapped at her stern and she could hardly be described as a thing of beauty. A freighter, of some ten thousand tons displacement though she looked much less. Cargo weight kept her hull low in the water and her name and port of origin on the stern were almost submerged. "*Dimitri Donskoi* – Leningrad".

The tug had started to edge the freighter round towards the estuary, the *Donskoi's* siren bellowed again, but there was no one on the launch who could hear her warnings. Again and again the whistles continued and the *Bully Boy* came on, like David's slingshot against Goliath.

"Drunken capitalist swine!" Janet imagined what the *Donskoi's* deck officers were probably thinking, and they were probably right, she supposed. Her uncle and Mackenzie and Peter Kent had once been capitalists, but they were dead now. No money, no finance or human orders could halt the *Bully Boy's* final effort.

She watched the launch reach her target. She saw the bow cut into the Russian's side, and that was all she saw for a long time. The Thames – London River, exploded.

Sixteen

"HOLOCAUST" – "WAVE FROM HELL" – "WALL OF WATER". Tom had been reading the newspapers and their treatment was dramatic; why not?

Thirty-eight people were killed when the *Bully Boy* blew up and there were over a hundred injured; half of them seriously. Apart from the *Donskoi*, which had been already declared a total loss, four other vessels were badly damaged. The tidal wave which followed had created havoc ashore, and the public were very angry. Everyone was most upset and the *Daily Globe* listed the aggrieved in order of importance.

The British and the Soviet Government – the Ministry of Health and the Home Office – the London Authorities (Outer and Inner) – the Thames Conservancy Board – the relatives and dependants of the victims – the Gas and Electricity Boards – the ship owners and the owners of property. All these bodies, their representatives and many more individuals were after blood and only two men stopped them getting it.

Mr Angus MacTamil QC had based his defence on temporary insanity, but Tom and Mott were not present to hear his opening address. They and Janet were in hospital at the time, though Kirk gave evidence.

"Yes, Mr MacTavish, I knew Simon Vale very well and was extremely fond of him," Kirk stated confidently in the witness box and then looked rather embarrassed, at the correction. "Ah, it's MacTamil, of course. Do apologize, sir, very foolish and rude of me.

"Now, as to your question." He paused again to consider it. "Difficult point for a man to answer when he's under oath, but I'll try to do my best.

"No, Mr MacTamil, it is not for me to swear whether Sir Simon was capable of running a vast business like A.C.E. but the results seem to speak for themselves." Tom imagined his bow to the judge and smirk at the jury. "Fifty shillings up, last Friday, my lord and ladies and gentlemen.

"However, though I know little about financial matters, I am a general officer and a former Commander of the British Army's Intelligence Corps, and those qualifications give me the right to speak on the subject of psychology. Here are the facts, as far as I know them." He clicked his heels and stared soulfully around the room. "A man of authority" – "a man you could trust" – "a true bulwark of Britain," were just a few of the reporters' comments.

"As Mr MacTamil has mentioned, Sir Simon Vale and his two deceased partners suffered horribly during the last world war. Three weeks in an open boat, during Arctic conditions. Could you stand such an ordeal, members of the jury?" He drew out a purple silk handkerchief and dabbed his eyes. "Well, probably not, and neither could I, but those men did. They never complained or grumbled. Not for one moment did despair cross their hearts. They stuck to the traditions of the service and . . .

"Oh, thank you, my lord. You are most kind and a seat would be very welcome." The judge had told the witness to sit down if he wished and Kirk lowered himself into a chair and groaned. "As your lordship and the jury have been informed, those men did not break. They came through their torment unscathed and more action followed." A gulp, a sob and another application of the handkerchief. "When hostilities ended, Sir Simon, Mr Kent and Mr MacDonald . . . I beg your pardon, sir." He frowned at counsel's interruption. "Do apologize – just a simple old soldier and tend to find Scottish names a bit repetitive at times, Mr MacTamil." According to the *Globe*, the simple soldier appeared bewildered by emotion and grief. "The third partner was William Mackenzie of course and he and his comrades started A.C.E. as soon as the European war was over. They had hardly any capital, very little experience, but somehow the business prospered."

Hardly any capital! Why was Kirk perjuring himself, Tom wondered, glancing at the newspaper. The simple soldier knew all about the Russian gold. He knew about the transactions in Tangiers. General Charlie knew just about damn near everything, so why had he lied to protect the good name of a man who had deserted his son?

"A good business, Mr MacCamel, and I use that adjective in every sense of the word." The handkerchief was raised once more, but this time to blow Kirk's nose. "Good for the investors, good for the staff and good for this our country too.

"Not a single strike or industrial dispute in almost forty years – quite a record." Kirk lifted a glass of water and drank deeply. "But years pass, as they do for us all, and Sir Simon Vale grew old and prepared for the great meeting with his Maker. We all know that explosives were lodged in the *Bully Boy's* hull, though to my own mind, for the most innocent reasons." The glass jangled as his shaking hand replaced it. "Sir Simon wished to die at sea and the detonation was intended to occur in deep water. And in complete safety, my friends, so what went wrong? What, indeed, went wrong? Who is to blame for the terrible tragedy which followed?" He faced the judge and gave another frank and slightly bitter smile. "I am, my lord. I, Major-General Charles Kirk, accept full responsibility." The *Globe's* text was interrupted by a photograph of the major-general staring soulfully towards the camera. "A Man of Courage", read the caption beneath it.

"Yes, I, members of the jury; foolishness, perversity, blind panic – call it what you like, but I am the culprit – the malefactor." The handkerchief was in use again and tears – real tears – trickled down Kirk's cheeks.

"When I heard that Miss Janet Vale, Sir Simon's niece, had been taken aboard that launch, I imagined the worst. I honestly believed that a mass suicide attempt could be in the offing and more, much more, was to follow.

"I voiced my foolish suspicions to Mr Thomas Mayne and to Mr J. Molden-Mott, the world famous explorer and they believed me. On my stupid orders and with great gallantry, they leapt off that bridge and boarded the yacht. Poor Mac-Intyre – Mackenzie, I mean – was crushed when Mayne fell on him and the unfortunate Peter Kent . . ." A sob, a gulp and a moment's silence. "Nobody knows what happened to Kent, but I – I do not ask for human mercy, ladies and gentlemen of the jury, though may the Great God, whom I worship, show pardon on a most repentant sinner."

"Why – why?" Tom spoke aloud. The article ended with a notice that the trial would continue tomorrow and he tossed the paper aside and paced the floor of his shop. "Why should Kirk behave in such a way? Why chop his own head off for nothing?"

"General Kirk's head is still firmly on his shoulders and it will remain there." Tom had imagined he was alone, but he stopped muttering and swung round as he heard the voice. "Why did he lie, Tom? Surely you can guess the reason? Money, of course, rather a lot of money. The major-general required his pound of flesh, but who cares?" Janet Vale smiled at him from the doorway. Her left arm was in a sling, plaster covered her right cheek, but Tom had never seen her look more lovely: vital, radiant and shining with happiness. "The case ended an hour ago, and though damages haven't been formally agreed, MacTamil feels sure that three million should settle the score. That's not including Jimmy and Kirk's costs naturally. They want full control of the firm. Ninety per cent of my holding, but what does that matter? I'll still be a moderately wealthy woman and A.C.E. will remain an independent concern, though under different management."

"Jimmy." The name conveyed nothing to Tom except Janet's acquaintance, the Honourable Stewart-Smith. "Where the hell does he fit in?"

"He was so wonderful, Tom. In spite of Jimmy's injuries, he limped into court at the final moments and confirmed everything that Kirk had said."

"Limped indeed! Fallen off another polo pony, I presume." Tom had heard that Stewart-Smith was liable to such accidents. "And what evidence had Jimmy to offer on Kirk's behalf?"

"Polo pony! What are you talking about, Tom?" Janet stepped forward and frowned at him. "Jimmy merely stated that he and Kirk were men of honour and integrity, and the judge fully agreed. He said that they were two of the finest gentlemen he had ever listened to, and no criminal charges would ever be preferred against them."

"Blimey!" Tom's mind reeled at the extent of human iniquity. "And Mr MacTamil QC promoted this scheme, I presume. He arranged for Kirk to go into the box and lie himself stupid."

"No, and do stop swearing and talking in clichés, Tom." Janet stamped her foot petulantly. "Kirk suggested the idea himself and Jimmy naturally backed him up. Why not?

"Why slander the dead? My uncle's body! Peter Kent and Mackenzie were blown to pieces by the explosion and the last copy of that damned book went with them.

"I know they were bad men once. Evil possibly, but regarded as heroes and benefactors by the general public. How can you discredit a benevolent hero without evidence, Tom? Why attempt to do so?" Janet suddenly looked really angry. "Peter Kent imagined that I wanted power. He also believed that I might be a bastard.

"Could be right, on the second point. I don't know, but I'm completely sure he was wrong on the first. Never had the slightest wish to control A.C.E. Something like this would be more my line of country." She looked around the shelves and frowned. "Been gathering a lot of dust in your absence, though that's no business of mine.

"But, does the name Sanity Fair mean anything to you, Tom?"

"Yes," he nodded. "Sanity Fair was a second-hand bookshop off the Edgeware Road kept by an insane young woman called Rosalie de Retz. Can't remember the details, but I think she went bust and committed suicide."

"Balls!" Janet fingered the pile of books she had bought from Mrs Rayner. "Rosalie was a friend of mine and she never killed herself. She slipped in front of a Number Nine bus when she was tight, and she had a thriving business and an excellent gimmick. It sometimes pays to be against things.

"Things that many people disapprove of, Tom." She considered his question. "Politicians and the H-Bomb – blood sports and the colour bar – capital punishment, class distinctions and the House of Lords.

"You name the pie, and Rosalie had a finger through its crust. Her shop was always full of well-meaning loonies, who paid a lot of money to foster their discontent.

"Got you." Janet had picked up the first volume of *Roger's Poetical Works* and twisted the cover slightly. Like a conjuring trick, the gilt edges faded and a landscape seemed to leap into focus. A brightly coloured picture of a farmhouse beside a stream with a line of blue hills stretching away in the background. The illustration had been made while the book was held bent in a vice and only became visible at its present angle.

"And let's see what the second volume has to offer. Ah, better still." Another twist and a group of nymphs and satyrs appeared. "Mildly erotic, and they're having a high old time on the grass. Well, Tom, few people may read Sam Rogers today, but everyone likes a good fore-edge painting. A pity they're not double-edged, but worth a damn sight more than I paid."

"At least ten times more." Tom felt extremely envious. "And I never spotted them. Your property, Janet, and you'd make a damned good bookseller."

"I think I might if anybody offered me a partnership, but those are yours." She pushed the books aside with a gesture of irritation. "What use are two heavy Victorian volumes to me, when Jimmy has asked for my hand in marriage?"

"Congratulations, my dear." Tom reluctantly decided that courtesy costs nothing. "And when will the happy union take place?"

"Next month at Saint Gloria's, Hanover Square, if we can

arrange it, providing Canterbury is available to take the service. Jimmy is such a wonderful man, you know. When I told him how neurotic I was about marriage – how I imagined that any man who proposed to me would be after my money – he just laughed. Said that as he and Kirk controlled the firm now, the problem no longer existed. Wasn't that clever, Tom?"

"Yes, extremely clever." Tom felt more than slightly sick. In his own mind he felt that the Honourable Mr Stewart-Smith could best be described as a right bastard.

"And so kind and thoughtful, too." Janet prattled on like a schoolgirl. "Jimmy says he's bound to be mentioned in the next honours list, and he has promised to adopt the title of Lord Vale. In that way we can keep the firm in the family tradition. His own name is far superior to ours of course, but . . ."

"But he just wanted to please you." Tom's voice snarled with contempt, but Janet seemed incapable of hearing criticism of her precious Jimmy.

"Yes, that's right, and doesn't it show what a fine and noble man he is?"

"It does indeed." Tom made a note in his diary. "St. Gloria's, Hanover Square, sometime next month." When the ceremony took place, he intended to be present and sling a few rocks at the bridegroom. "Any date fixed yet?"

"No. That depends on the Archbishop being available, of course. I wanted a very simple service, but Jimmy said he had a debt to his public image. Archbishops come and go, but his name will live on forever."

"Public image?" Tom couldn't imagine what Stewart-Smith's image might be. Perjury in court – fraudulent conversion – being drunk in charge of a motor car or a polo pony, came to mind, but they were hardly adequate.

"Yes, and the honeymoon afterwards; that will be exciting." Janet's eyes glowed. "We're going to build a replica of that salvage tug, the *Sam*, and sail off to raise the *Titanic*."

"The devil you are!" Once again, an image flitted through Tom's head, and he saw the beautiful Janet Vale, though she was beautiful no longer. Janet looked wan and wrinkled and she was clad in oilskins. She was operating a pump to send oxygen down to Mr Jimmy Stewart-Smith.

No, he was wrong! He had to be wrong, and Stewart-Smith played no part in the picture. A very different figure dangled pompously in the replica's diving bell.

"Janet," he said. "You can't – you don't mean – Mott?"

"Of course, I do; who else? Jimmy Molden-Mott. Didn't you know that his Christian name is James?"

"No, I didn't know that. I didn't know that there is anything Christian about him, but you can't marry Mott, Janet. The man's a brute, a boor and a human monster . . ." He broke off and saw the laughter in her face.

"No, of course I can't," she said. "But there's only one thing that will stop me.

"Yes, Tom," she started to say. "If you want to save me from a fate worse than death, you'll have to . . ." She tried to say, but broke off as he opened his arms and came towards her.

There was really nothing more to be said.

www.ingramcontent.com/pod-product-compliance
Lightning Source LLC
Chambersburg PA
CBHW011750010726
47498CB00012B/3006